A Slow Fall

Mark Ayling

Foreword

The grey waves churned, and a small boat struggled insignificantly shoreward. Alistair Darling, still not fully recovered from the accident, was circumspect and worried. The wind flapped against his face like a trapped bird beating itself to death on a windowpane, and sand snarled around his ankles. Margaret seemed oblivious to these omens as she collected shells in a plastic bag; crouching and straightening, her trousers rode up to reveal pale and stubbly skin that reminded Ally of badly plucked poultry.

Seagulls squabbled amongst themselves and appeared beaten into an iron sky as heraldic symbols on a shield. One by one, they spiralled down to land with a little jump. A red pinprick had appeared on Maggie's jacket and moved around annoyingly; surely there weren't insects this time of year? Ally made to brush the dot away, but it scooted effortlessly over the back of his hand. He tried to pick it off, but each time his fingers fumbled and missed it.

High up on the cliff, a man with an arm like a boned piglet squinted through his telescopic sight. In front of him, a book of handwritten poems had fallen open at the page *Uncle Cyril and Auntie Phyllis were Swingers*. The scanning crosshairs momentarily paused to watch the seagulls leave muddy imprints as primitive as bow and arrow etchings on a cave wall.

Ally flicked at the red spot with ever more urgent motions, yet each time it rode serenely over his strokes and the contempt on Maggie's face was obvious. The hat and scarf he'd carefully arranged that morning to keep the wind off his chest, now made him feel trapped and unable to breathe.

Suddenly there was the sound of a stone thudding into mud. Except it wasn't a stone. Maggie stumbled and her bag fell to the floor spilling the shells she had painstakingly collected. A shockingly crimson worm emerged from her nose; it was the same colour as her lipstick. She dropped to her knees. Ally couldn't work out what was going on. Should he get help? But there wasn't anyone around, just the sand that circled ever more frantically. As her eyes locked with his, he glimpsed deep within them dark roiling waves like the oceans of a fading planet on which the last solitary creature was dying alone.

Chapter 1

The silver rods of rain relentlessly spun down the street like the spokes of a bicycle wheel, and businessmen dashed from doorway to doorway. The chrome rain splintered across their shoulders as if they'd just collided and mangled with that self-same bicycle. The younger ones ploughed forward remorselessly with the strength and stamina of people who worked out regularly. Ally knew that was what fascism taught the world, that the physically perfect were pitiless. Maggie could be cold too, even if she was on the dumpy side. For example, when they passed a Big Issue seller, she would silently dare him to buy one and confirm her suspicions that he lacked backbone.

Ally was attempting to hail a cab. Yet another one had swept past, and he turned up his collar so as not to let his frustration show. A bald man and a giggling blonde appeared next to him.

They were drunk and Ally had the impression they would make love later. She was pretty in an antidepressant-dependant way and his baldness seemed to fit him like an overstretched swimming cap. Ally tried to picture them locked together but all that came to mind was the image of a fat man on a unicycle; the unsteady progress and flesh folded over the frame like damp bedding put out to dry.

Despite this, Alistair Duncan and Margaret Hoffa both enjoyed the moment. They were enveloped by the warmth of the bald man's wealth. Fleetingly, it seemed to protect them from the fumes, noise and misery in a perfumed bubble. And as the orange and red taillights from the cars milled in the tarmac like koi, Ally could imagine him and Maggie somewhere far way, somewhere thrilling and full of adventure. Shanghai or Macau.

Eventually, a black cab cut across the traffic and headed towards them with the nasal and rasping effort of a charging hippo. Success! He was elated and even stood a little taller as if for once he had got one over on the self-satisfied rich. He opened the door and turned with a flourish to Maggie, but before she could move, fatso and bimbo jumped in. The door was snatched from his hand and the taxi sped away sucking all the warmth and laughter with it. Ally was left at the kerbside of a dismal London street, raising his hand again as ineffectually as he had at school. Maggie dug her elbow hard into his ribs.

After that, taxis came and went, but each time Alistair had less conviction. He edged further into the road, his arm stretching as if it was being wrenched from its socket. Ally felt the tug on his coat as cars sped by. Tyres sounded like material ripping, and the tear seemed to be getting nearer by the minute. Ally stood on tiptoe, he reached, he hailed, took another step, and then at his limit, Alistair Duncan was suddenly propelled forwards. Brakes squealed, horns blared and a blackness as dark and sticky as fountain-pen ink poured into his nose and mouth.

***

Ally woke in hospital. He slept and woke many times, but sleeping was nicer. Nurses came and went. The catheter inflamed his penis. He sipped water and ate rice pudding that reminded him of school and pink custard. One day when he got up on unsteady legs and stood in front of the sink, he discovered his forehead was dented like a boiled egg tapped with a teaspoon. The nurses smiled as they passed. Vera was Lithuanian and perched on his bed. He told her about the time he had a kidney infection, and the Indian GP who worked away at a computer so ancient the screen fizzed with green radiation. It had beeped each time an entry was refused. And it had beeped a lot. Yet he'd kept jabbing away at the keyboard like a crow pecking at roadkill. The room had looked as temporary as a time-share sales office, and on the only bookshelf there were holiday brochures and a

9

single book. Ally'd had to tilt his head sideways to read the title, *Be Your Own Lawyer.*

"No sheet," Vera said.

"Yes shit."

"A sued man is a kareful von," Vera said as she got up, smoothing her dress.

"I don't suppose a few textbooks would've gone amiss," Ally said to himself before slipping into sleep again.

Days went by. No one came to visit. Vera, pronounced Wera, had big tits and when she leant over to adjust his pillows, they would nudge his cheek like inquisitive ponies. She had good posture and carried her breasts like a skilled waitress would a drinks tray.

Ally had concluded that being in hospital must be similar to being on a cruise, though he hadn't experienced either before. There were a lot of white things, endless empty days and too many old people. And when a nurse came, it was a brief relief from the monotony, like entering port; *Cadiz from 3 to 5, be back or miss departure.*

The evening of his accident, they'd been to the theatre. Maggie had brought a hip flask of Zubrowka and drank most of it herself. At one point, she'd pressed his hand up her skirt, grinding her hips so his fingers had bent over. A week later, he took his clothes from the locker and left the hospital. They hadn't been washed and blood caked the collar. His mobile phone and wallet were missing, and it amazed him how easily his past had been thoroughly erased.

***

Everything was too quick and his brain was buffering the information. At the traffic lights, he crossed with the children and pensioners, it was in this company he felt safe. Ally wanted a fluorescent bib and yellow hat and to be singing *The wheels of the bus go around and around.*

When he reached his flat, his heart was beating in a heavy and loose way. Through the door, Ally could hear music and a shower running. He pressed his forehead against the cool surface as if somehow he would pass through if only he maintained the pressure long enough. By the way the water fell unevenly, he could tell someone had stepped under it, interrupting the flow. It's how he had felt most of his life, an unwanted impediment to other people's relentless momentum. He rang the bell. Maggie took a long time answering the door and when she did, it was amid a swirl of steam.

"Where the hell have you been?" she said.

Her legs were the colour of prawns and looked freshly shaved. She was an irregular shaver and rarely took a shower, but today she looked soft and poached.

"I've not been well."

"You were OK when I last saw you showing off to that blonde slut."

"Bruising," Ally said making a vague gesture like a magician introducing his assistant.

"But then that's just like you, disappearing when I need you most."

"Vera says I look like a Friesian cow."

"And don't think you're coming in."

She slammed the door in his face.

There may have been hushed voices from within, but it could just have easily been the TV. The door flew open, and Maggie emerged from an even bigger cloud like a reality star unexpectedly recalled to the show.

"That's it?"

Was she expecting flowers?

"You can fuck off right now."

Where should he fuck off to?

As if reading his mind, she added, "I'm sure that bum chum in combat fatigues would have you. Two weirdos together, just perfect."

"Who?" Ally said, but he knew. He only had one friend.

"Spasiod."

Bum chum? Spasoid? He hadn't heard these words since primary school and even then, only by those in the special set that everyone feared. Ally must've been shaking his head as she continued.

"Village idiot guy!"

"People."

"Eh?"

"Village People guy, not idiot."

"I know what I mean," she said slamming the door.

In truth, Jon had a liking for leather chaps and house makeover programmes, yet he was as emaciated as a Bangkok rat.

He didn't know how long he stood there, and he ached as he recalled the smell of her neck. Time had become strange and abstract with the past more real than the present, and the hospital seemed like paradise with its harsh florescent lighting and buxom angels bringing him apple crumble. Maybe he should go back there, take off his clothes and climb back into the bed as if he'd only popped out for a smoke and now was ready to comply with the rules once again. Just as he was about to leave, the door was suddenly yanked back open.

"I can't believe you did what you did."

She was almost shouting, and Ally feared the neighbours he only ever nodded to the past 10 years would come to the door.

"I'm standing there in the sodding rain and out of nowhere my husband is across the road staring at me. The psycho bastard is actually there, in front of us. I run but of course when I look around, you're nowhere to be seen. You disappear like the wimp you are. Where the hell had you gone anyway, slobbering after that fat pussy?"

There were red blotches on her chest.

"The least you could've done is bloody well call, but oh no not you. A mobile is kryptonite to you. You'd rather have a prostate examination than use the phone. And who the fuck is Vera?"

When the door shut this time, it was with a rush of wind that was like a tube train hurtling past and sucking the air from the station.

Fat pussy? What could she mean by that?

Chapter 2

It wasn't coming together and hadn't been for months, years probably. Sometimes even the smell of the paint sickened him. It was only the emptiness of not doing it that kept him going. Alcohol, sleeplessness and cigarettes coalesced to form the shadowy lands he inhabited. Greg considered himself a figure in a half-developed negative from bygone times, which no one (no matter how hard they tried) could quite make out. He could've easily been a farmer, Quaker, apoplectic squire, or even a two-bit whore. They were all equally possible.

There'd been some minor success early on, or rather a few sales to friends who secretly pitied him. This was primarily down to the ferocity of his application which masked a mediocrity he'd never admit, even to himself. There was no ease or grace, and he needed anger and harshness to bring his paintings to life. Maggie was always turned away in his paintings, as he feared the mutilation of his brushstrokes. He could never get her hands right either. The fingers were pink and bald. Huddled together, they were an unhappy and runt-ish litter. The line of a song had stuck in his mind, *You weren't much of a muse but then I wasn't much of a poet*. Well, that was them, Gregory and Margaret.

***

"You'll never believe what just happened," Maggie was saying before she was through the door. "He just turns up at the flat looking like a beat up nonce, plaster over one eye and cotton wool in his ear."

She flopped in the sagging armchair and glanced around. But almost immediately, she was up again pacing the studio as if sizing it for furniture.

"Was he wearing a duffle coat?"

"Eh?"

"Drink?"

"Vodka. No ice, no water, no nothing. Just more vodka." Maggie paused briefly to watch Greg fill her glass to the brim. "Apart from that there was barely a scratch on him. He's like a Power Ranger, bullets just ping off him."

"Which one?"

"Which one what?"

"Which Power Ranger?"

"How the hell should I know?" she said, sipping her drink so as not to spill any. "Nobody over the age of twelve knows who any of them are."

"My favourite is Dynamo."

Were all men children? One way or another all women knew they would be changing nappies for the rest of their life. The butts just got hairier. There always came a point when the men in Maggie's life sucked in their gut, flexed a weedy bicep and she was compelled to say something like, 'I guess you been working out, uh?'

19

"Do bullets ping off him?" Maggie said with a sigh.

"You arranged for him to be shot as well?"

"Like Rasputin?"

"I don't know that one," Greg said. "Was that for the eastern Europe market?"

"Are you mentally subnormal?"

Greg made coffee. He liked this bit the most about being a painter. Not the actual painting but the stuff that comes with it. The turpentine and coffee fumes, smoke twisting from his cheroot like elvers. He'd always been amazed how easily women had been impressed by this black Mass of wine and incense. He was sure one day they would see through it, denounce him for the fraud he was and hang him from the city walls in a sack. The espresso jug sizzled on the hob and more brown spatters added to the ones that already dappled the enamel. It was his piebald cooker and Greg patted it as if it had carried him safely through a desert. Two years in the planning and now things were finally moving. Admittedly not smoothly, but he could make adjustments along the way.

"There's something not right with him," Maggie said, holding up her glass to watch the oily liquid. It looked as if he'd cleaned his brushes in it.

"Now she notices."

"No, more than usual. Something in the eyes, or rather something not there. It's as if the nudge button has come up flashing and he needs a good punch to the head," Maggie finished her drink like a toast at a Mafia wedding, "and free everything up."

"That deaf, dumb and blind kid sure plays a shit pinball," lifting the pot lid, Greg watched the coffee swirl like a backed-up latrine, "due mainly to his sensory deprivation."

"You think this is funny?"

He sat down, crossed his legs and lit a cigarette, "Well, yes."

She was staring vacantly at his canvasses. He couldn't tell if she noticed not much progress had been made.

"Are you sure he has it?"

After two long years, of course, he was sure. It'd been his one and only exhibition and Fran had walked in off the street looking mad and wasted. The thing that threw him most were her lips, they were the same colour as her skin like manikins have. Greg had paid to rent a pop-up shop in the high street for a week, never telling Maggie he'd used their savings to do so.

He'd taped his canvasses to the blue partitions which gave off the depressing feel of a Health and Safety seminar at the borough offices. He'd covered the table with a duvet slip, laid out the newly printed business cards, flipped over the closed/open sign and waited.

But no one came in, not even the rain bothered to poke its head in. There was more life on bingo night at the hospice. Chingford pensioners just didn't seem to be interested in art; cat food, tinned sardines and tomatoes in a polythene bag, they liked. But not art. He watched them hobble past, the bitterness in their faces colder than any gulag winter. Greg wanted to throw open the door and scream into the street, 'Tomatoes are not the only fruit!' No, they weren't interested in anything that wasn't embossed, glowed in the dark, or had a photo of an animal with an amusingly long tongue and accompanying innuendo-laden caption.

Once a couple had half-opened the door thinking it a coffee shop, but when they realised their mistake, they fell over themselves backing away. It was as if they'd nearly entered the opium den of tattooed prostitutes just waiting to seduce them with the mystical ways of the Orient. It was then that the futility of his venture had fully dawned on Greg. After all, how could these people – who'd experienced nothing more exotic than Leyton Orient on a Saturday afternoon and ate food that looked like a sneeze on a plate – possibly understand art?

Was it chance that brought Fran to his door that very day? Or had fate intervened, realising he'd had about enough as any man could take and decided to throw him a lifeline? He was closing up when Fran and had breezed in. If these two insignificant events hadn't occurred on the same day, Greg doubted he would be set on the course he was now. This was why he knew none of this, or what may happen in the future, could possibly be his fault. Walking straight past his paintings and without giving them a second glance, she'd lit a damp cigarette and looked him in the eye. It wasn't long before he knew all about the sappy ex-husband she kept returning to when she needed money or a bed.

The pot on the stove gurgled and spat. Greg topped up Maggie before addressing the coffee. He discarded the dregs in his mug with the same motion a person would use to get a reluctant biro to work and poured fresh in.

"We've been through this a thousand times," he said over his shoulder.

"I know," she sighed, "but it's not you that has to put up with his molesting and slobbering advances. It's like kissing the palsied kid at local disco who's come in his pants before he's got your bra off."

"Hey, hey. I know," Greg said but was secretly shocked by her language and what she might be doing. "You're practically Mother Teresa, Gandhi and the Pope all in one but with a better moisturising regime."

"Hold me," she said.

He gestured to the coffee in his hand. Greg had paused in front of one of his abandoned canvasses, "Perhaps figurative art isn't the way forward anymore."

"What?"

"You see a lot of words in paintings now. Graffiti is big. Think Banksy."

"The writing's on the wall for graffiti," she said absently.

He glanced over, but she wasn't smiling. Maggie had always been sharp, at ease with talents he was amazed by and envied. She was drinking as smoothly and systematically with the glazed trance of a weightlifter doing reps well within his range.

"How's the painting going?" she said.

"Just peachy."

When she left, he took a knife and stabbed the canvas again and again.

***

There is a physical diminishing that comes with brain injury, like rapid ageing. Ally felt he was blackening and shrivelling like something that only vegans would eat. Accompanying this was a tentativeness. It was hard to place the feeling exactly but how he thought of it was that it was like spending time with himself as a child. He had become a child in an old man's body, but these entities somehow remained separate and talked to each other. Each caring for the other but neither really liking the other. They even feared each other a little. He thought it must be like being either the product of some gone-wrong scientific experiment or one of the Rolling Stones.

A memory had recently come back to him from decades ago. It was bonfire night and he was in the back garden with his dad. Ally had a sparkler in his hand and when he waved it around left a luminous trail on his retina like a light-bulb filament. Despite the intervening years, it felt like yesterday, how the fireworks made colourful palm trees in the sky and down in the town the face of St Anthony's Church was illuminated from below, hollowing out its features. Afterwards, they'd both stood staring up at the stars, it had been a moment they'd shared. But Ally had soon become terrified by the sheer enormity of the universe, and he'd been unable to explain to anyone why he was suddenly crying.

***

The miner's lamp strapped to Jon's forehead made its own low-watt pyrotechnic display as it skittered across the wall and ceiling. They were watching back-to-back episodes of Come Dine with Me, and Ally used his hand to clear his rheumy eyes. Jon said he had the look of a dog that only vaguely understood it was dying.

"This guy's meant to be a hairdresser but see how his hands are shaking," Jon said, the coin of light spinning like an out-of-control alien spacecraft crashing into the unwashed dishes and paramilitary paraphernalia.

"I wouldn't trust him with my sack, crack and back."

"Do they offer that at Greek Tony's?" Ally said, suddenly unable to shake the unwanted mental picture of Jon bent over a red leatherette chair with its chrome, height-adjusting foot pump.

"He's doing monkfish wrapped in Parma ham for main, followed by crème brûlée for pudding."

Jon was waiting for Armageddon or a deadly virus to zombie-fy the world. He was convinced that with his Swiss Army knife and matches dipped in wax, he would assume natural command of the remaining few. Ally's dad had matches like that for fishing and kept them in an old metal cigar holder, but he'd never known him to need them. The curtains were never opened on Jon and Ally's existence together which had taken on a faded, sepia tone. All that was missing was from the tableau was a slow-ticking clock and a suicide.

***

Maggie had reached an age where her skin was just about to lose its lustre. Sometimes she had it, others not. The hand-mirror was the size of a ping pong bat and had coloured glass and whelk shells around the edge. It lay face down on the dressing table as if she couldn't bear to see what was lurking in there. It had been her mother's, and it was she who seemed to stare critically back at Maggie nowadays as if through a portal from the other side. When she was alive, there had been the endless calls and now, like ethereal Skyping, she was still getting through. Maggie had the feeling if she stared too long into the mirror, it would set, trapping her in some sort of ectoplasm gel the same consistency as a solidifying egg.

　　She knew this was her last chance, Maggie was a hoarder but men she couldn't keep. The flat was full of crap. Broken shelves and wonky tables, skip-rubbish, dying pot plants, even a bread-maker dragged all the way from Bethnal Green. She just couldn't help herself. Her other defining characteristics were never giving up, nor being wrong. So, when she went over the plan again in her head looking for the flaw, she just couldn't see it.

Chapter 3

Constable Sargit fumbled with his notepad as the WPC with the stout hips perched on the edge of an armchair. They'd both declined tea.

"Your wife…" Sarge began.

"Ex-wife."

He flipped a page over on his notebook and then back again, as if suddenly doubting a long-held belief. Ally wondered why they didn't have iPads, it seemed a quaint but inefficient way for going about things. Maybe the officer should have a cape and nightstick?

"Your ex-wife is missing."

This wasn't news to Ally, she often went AWOL. On benders she would turn up when the money or men ran out. Slumped comatose in a bar, custody suite or psychiatric unit, there would eventually be a call to come and get her.

Ally waited.

Sarge exchanged looks with the WPC. She had a good physique for hockey. Ally guessed there was probably lots of squatting and firm leverage involved in both hockey and policing which would build a meaty sort of strength that years of bad living wouldn't easily erode. She looked as though she might be popular down the social club.

"You don't seem particularly concerned."

"I'm not."

WPC Rebecca stood and left the room. Ally could hear her moving about in the bedroom. Doors opening. Draws. He didn't know why they were searching Jon's flat. Luckily, Jon was down at the Happy Shopper else he would've been citing jurisprudence like a soapbox preacher with one hand tucked in his breeches and the other clutching a Gideon New Testament.

"You didn't report her missing."

"I didn't know, Detective," Ally said.

"Constable."

"Sarge?" Rebecca's voice came through from the other room.

"Sarge Constable?" Ally said.

"Constable Sarge," he said taking the pen top from his mouth as if some conclusion had been silently arrived at. He'd been chewing it like a marmoset – angling his head to the side and using back teeth to work the little arm until it stood out to the side.

"Like in Catch 22?"

"Eh?"

Faces drifted by on the muted TV – some Ally recognised, most not. They seemed strangely bloated as if after a lunchbreak Botox. Maybe it needed re-tuning, but what setting would need adjusting to make people appear thinner or less dead?

"She's done this before," Ally said. "You must have records of that. I'm not in contact. I don't know where she is. I've been ill. Hospitalized." Ally pointed vaguely to his head.

Sarge shut his notebook and stood.

The WPC came waving a large artificial cock before her like the baton ready to pass to the next runner.

"Are you a homo?"

Ally couldn't shake the image of the marital toy the female officer had found, and it moved through his thoughts nightmarishly like a gently humming zeppelin. Were they all that big? Could it possibly be Jon's? Ally didn't feel comfortable – it was like knowing there was a mouse in the room crawling upside down along the curtains like a burglar in a black and white film. No adult crawled upside down nowadays, Ally thought.

It was only after a couple of days that he managed to find some sort of acceptance; postulating that it was most likely an anti-personnel device packed with C4 (Ally had a notion it could be moulded like plasticine). Trying to figure out what mechanism could be used to trigger such a device, he came up with several solutions. The simplest of which was a match inserted into the end and then when activated, it would vibrate and strike against an abrasive material. Although there were a few technical details to iron out, Ally felt he had grasped the concept of the IED in general terms. This brought him a degree of comfort.

*****

Ally's ex-wife perched naked on the bed picking fluff from her navel. She hadn't washed and there was an odour about her.

"Maggie says that since his head injury he's like some sort of screwed-up mystic. He smiles, doesn't rile, you can do anything you want to him." The sun fanned through the Venetian blinds like a hand of cards.

"Tweak the tiger's nose, and he won't do anything."

Fran ignored him as she worked bits of loose flesh at her waist, squeezing it until the blood drained away. Greg was disgusted by both her and himself.

"Maybe he's a prophet?" she said.

"But more likely he's a complete loss."

As soon as he got the money, he would rid himself of all the women in his life. They held him back, Greg knew this to be a caste-iron certainty. He dreamt of Paris. That's where he would be able to paint. Live the life. Drink the wine. Screw the women. It would be like *Last Tango in Paris*, although it was all rather vague apart from the butter scene. Maggie liked butter, but not in the same way. She ate huge chunks of it, and it made him sick. It was as if she was chewing a 500g bogey.

Greg padded through to the kitchen like an exhausted marsupial scratching its overhanging belly. He could make out Fran through the crinkled glass; however, rather than disassembling her face the glass seemed to put the fractured pieces back into their rightful place.

"The drugs I'm on," she called out, "make me indiscriminately horny."

"I don't need drugs for that," Greg said, but in reality, could've done with some.

Despite it being in the plan, Greg couldn't help the doubts that rose periodically to the surface. On the few occasions he'd been abroad, he had hated it. The sneering waiters made him lose confidence in skills he had mastered by the age of ten. Like handling money and communicating. The only other British he saw were pensioners usually trudging behind tour guides like downcast pit ponies, their wills broken. They looked as if they couldn't wait for the first drink or snooze of the day. Surely it couldn't be worth the unspoken contract they'd all made to spend the most vital years of life in dreary offices or workshops and end up with this? He knew having what you've always wanted brings despair.

No, he wouldn't end up like this, without vitality or will. Abroad for him would be hairy-legged women smoking cheroots with lipstick collared ends who would let loose viperous trails as they tilted their heads back. And he forced down his fears the same way one man would drown another, with his face turned aside as the water thrashed like in a shark attack.

Later, after getting rid of Fran on some pretext or other, Greg settled down to drink. He set about this in the same professional manner others would apply to a day's work. He lined up the bottle, glass and ice, turned off his mobile and locked the front door. The open window let the sounds of the outside world in: a woman's heels clipped with the speed of a 1950's touch-typist, a dog making a repetitive hollow sound, and the wind rattling shop shutters like riot police charging their shields. Methodically, Greg went over his plan as a blind man would braille text. Each detail was examined minutely with a budgerigar's head-cocked concentration, terrified he would miss something important.

Chapter 4

"By rights, I should've had a nuclear-biological warfare suit in there. I feel so damn itchy, I swear to God the carpet moved by itself, and there were these pants on the bed that were crusty."

Rebecca was off on one while Sarge tried to concentrate on the report.

"I mean, if I'd held them in a corner, they would've stuck out straight. He must be an Olympic standard wanker."

"I don't need to see his underwear to know that," Sarge said absently as his fingers plonked over the keyboard as if attempting chopsticks. He was slumped in the swivel chair, and it wasn't going well. Rebecca was leaning against his desk and when she shifted position, her stockings rustled. His groin stiffened.

"He bloody did it."

"When I tried to put the cock down," Rebecca said, "it stuck to my glove. I had to shake it loose. It was like the bloody thing was holding on."

Sarge wondered what it would be like to lift her heavy breasts out of her bra. He thought they would spill over his hand like softening ice cream. Straightening up, he resolved to set to his task with more vigour, but almost immediately his screen went blank.

"Shit... could you?"

He made room for her, and she squatted in front of him. Her bra was visible through the blouse and the top of a black thong showed over her skirt. The motion was easy for her, there was no knee cracking. As she moved the mouse, she bobbed a little as if encouraging a reluctant horse into a canter. Soon she was back on the table.

"There."

Sarge squinted and leant close.

"The pervert did it, and I'm going to get him. He murdered her," Sarge said, his finger hovered searching for the *q*, but it didn't seem to be anywhere on the keyboard. "He probably cut her up and ate her innards like calamari in front of the Antiques Roadshow." Suddenly the *q* emerged from the swirling letters, and he pressed it with delight. "I bet there are other victims too, the heads lined up in the fridge with chimpanzee grins and wispy hair like a row of gonks."

Rebecca smoothed her skirt.

"I kept the cock."

He stopped typing, "Eh?"

"The cock, I got it in my handbag."

"Why?"

"DNA."

"For the putting on or taking off?"

***

Maggie cleaned the flat. It helped her think. Doing order, she called it. The rug hung on the line, and she had beaten it to within an inch of its life. Everything was now in a worse mess than before she started. The cupboards were empty, and her clothes lay across the floor.

She'd tried to call Brain Dead but it kept going to answer phone, then she remembered his mobile had gone clattering across the tarmac when he went under the taxi. Why wasn't he as easily disposable as his bloody Nokia, and who the hell still used them apart from drug dealers and conspiracy theory nuts? What use was a phone you could only make calls on? In fact, the whole thing was such a cock up that she was having serious doubts about any of it.

Did Duncan really have any money? She'd never seen any evidence of any in all the time she'd known him. The cheapskate restaurants, the bus rides like they were a couple of pensioners, his best clothes out of style for a decade. How could Greg be so certain? True, he didn't have to put up with the slobbering and pawing like a St Bernard attempting to revive a downed skier, as she did. Yet they both knew his paintings were amateurish and worthless, the whole world could see that, so in reality, he had as much at stake as she did. More even. And he was so sure of his information.

'Yes, babe, I've got solid intel. One hundred percent. Don't ask. I have it from the horse's mouth.'

As she went about her cleaning and ordering, she waited for Ally. Maggie knew he would turn up sooner or later. It was just a matter of time. She played through in her head how she would handle it. Not like before. Maybe hold him, say she missed him. But the very thought of it made her skin crawl. Or she could make a joke of it? Ask should they go out somewhere, take a taxi? That was her making up, but would he realise that? He'd been so spaced out before. Probably the painkillers. Or was he really transformed? She'd told Greg he was. Like an epiphany. Maybe he'd seen a burning bush, levitating Madonna, or even a guardian angel – one that stood at his shoulder like in Wings of Desire. But not resigned and forbearing as in the film, but a vicious bastard with yellow eyes, a gull's screech and blood-spattered plumage. One that would know exactly her tardy soul.

***

There was a commotion on the TV. The water churned and men in wetsuits were struggling to master skittish craft. Helicopter blades smoothed the sea like the saggy skin of a weight-loss champion.

Jon was spooning cornflakes mechanically into his mouth.

"Pilot whales," he slurped through the mush, indicating with his spoon and at the same time giving Ally a benediction of semi-skimmed, "run aground again."

"Oh."

"Whoever called them that was having a bloody laugh."

***

The doorbell rang.

Maggie licked her lips, reached into her T shirt and tweaked her nipples. Steeling herself, she opened the door. Sarge stood there gawping at her sticky-out tits as Rebecca pushed round them and into the flat.

Sarge mumbled, "Police."

"The uniform sort of gave it away," Maggie said, pulling her cardigan together and crossing her arms.

Rebecca had snapped her gloves on and was already opening and closing drawers. Was she collecting dildos, Sarge thought?

There was a brief and awkward mingling as in a village hall disco before Sarge chose an

47

uncomfortable-looking chair and crossed his legs.
Washing was drying on the doors and backs of
chairs and the smell of washing powder hung in the
damp air. Freshly laundered sheets had always
evoked faintly erotic feelings within him.

"We have reason to believe a serious crime
has taken place."

Maggie paced up and down, maybe Ally
wasn't so brain-damaged after all. She'd been there,
true, but she hadn't pushed him. Maggie would say
that. Say she was spooked and didn't even realize
he'd taken a dive under the car. She would say they
were just friends but he wanted more. Was
practically a stalker. Was it her responsibility, she
was only the lodger?

"Tea?" Maggie asked, picking at a loose
thread from her cardigan. As she pulled, it seemed
to have extraordinary length. Then she noticed pair
of slippers poking out from under the G plan and
these, too, she thought looked like accident victims.
She needed to pull herself together.

"Do you know a Mr Alistair Duncan?"

"Of course, I bloody do. He's my landlord," she said and added unnecessarily, "I'm only here 'cos the rent's cheap. Through a friend, I was desperate and had no choice. It's temporary. I don't know him. Not really."

Sarge thought maybe he should be making notes of this, but he couldn't help wondering what it would be like to live with a woman that wasn't your mother. A world full of sensations: pants drying on a clotheshorse, lipstick imprints on cup rims, and the heavy scent of shampoo trailing from room to room.

Rummaging sounds were coming from the bedroom.

"Is your colleague alright in there?"

Sarge glanced up. Whatever Rebecca was doing, she was making heavy work of it. There were dull thuds like the chopping of wood.

"Can you describe his movements recently?"

49

"Regular."

"Eh?"

"Has a lot of fibre and accompanying flatulence."

"Physical not bowel."

"Slow and stiff then. He's definitely no Anton du Beke."

"Are you trying to be funny?"

"If I try, usually I'm not, and if I don't, I am." When she was nervous, Maggie's mouth often got her into trouble. "I'm not trying now, so probably I am. But I hadn't noticed. In fact, no one usually notices."

Maggie knew it wasn't a good to be a smart ass with the police, but she couldn't help herself. She was winding the thread round her fingers now, drawing it tightly so it left a bright red mark.

"It appears Mr Duncan's been involved in an incident."

Sarge was losing what little control he had over the situation and a tremor went through his muscles like someone who had over-exerted themselves. Then out of nowhere, Maggie was talking at ten to the dozen, "He fell, wasn't pushed, not that I saw. It's fucked up his head. It's damaged. His head doesn't work right." She drew a breath, "He can't remember things. I wasn't even there. Well, I was but not at the time. I had already left."

Bath foam also excited him, and he wondered whether it was a cleanliness thing or a mother thing. He hoped to hell it was the former.

"You know he's a bloody naturist?" Maggie knew she couldn't stop herself. The brakes had failed on her mouth, which was now a runaway, "Sometimes he walks round here with it all hanging out. Put me off giblets for life. I had to tell him to stop or I was moving out. He took me to a beach in Norfolk once which was a cross between Hieronymus Bosh and Saga Holidays."

Sarge scrawled the word 'sick' in his pad and underlined it three times.

Rebecca came back in and winked at him. There was a bulge in her trouser pocket. He looked at his crumpled notebook and the single word he'd written there. There was silence and everyone was looking at him. Suddenly, Sarge stuffed the book in his jacket pocket and, with all the bravado he could muster, announced, "We've reason to believe Mr Duncan killed his wife."

"He did it," Maggie said without hesitation.

Chapter 5

The same disease moved in Sarge as in his brother. Only slower. The TS didn't show yet; it worked away quietly. Sometimes, he imagined it seeding over the surface of his brain like tiny mushrooms growing in the half-light, drawing nutrients from the guano. At times, he was sure he felt them nudging up and unfurling their smooth heads. A soft army of death. He looked it up once in Wikipedia and it said how tuberoses sclerosis feasted on the soft internal organs, and it made him think of plump Leopold Bloom tucking a napkin under his chin and sitting down to dinner. In his brother, it was hungrier, though; its appetite was ferocious more like Hannibal Lector.

Last year, Sarge had been offered a bride from Kashmir. She was over forty and looked after her brother's six children. She didn't speak English and he didn't speak Urdu. When he met her, she was squatting on the floor and it looked as if her bottom-half was dangling through the ceiling of the basement below. No one squatted in his family, they used chairs like everyone else. She had big hands and although he couldn't see them, he presumed she had big feet too. Sarge imagined her gliding from room to room, her toes working away furiously like a bank teller counting notes.

Maybe there was a genetic advantage to big extremities, probably on a farm breach-birthing stock or hefting an axe. And during rainy season, they would displace an equal mass of water according to the third law of something or other. What were the other two laws anyway? Did anyone know? Sarge had to admit there was most likely an evolutionary advantage in the Hindu Kush, but not in East London. Despite this, the thought of a wife – even a clod-hoping one like Olive Oyl – had given him a certain frisson. But she never came back for a second viewing and wasn't mentioned again. He wasn't offered another one.

***

Maggie had given up waiting after the police visit and called Jon on what he called the 'bat phone'. Jon would refer to his 'secret and secure line' that was so secret no one knew about it. In reality, it was a pay-as-you-go mobile on which he still had the same £5 credit for the last ten years.

It'd taken Jon some time to recognise the tinny rendition of Metallica's *Here comes the Sandman* coming from his groin was actually the phone ringing.

"Who the fuck is this and how did you get this number?"

"Just put him on, saddo."

***

Jon drove, changing gear, cutting the traffic, talking to Ally and rolling a cigarette all at the same time. Ally tried to count his arms and legs, there seemed too many like an alien losing its grip on human form. But not one from the erratic disc, they would obviously be too small.

"Are you sure you want to do this?" Jon picked tobacco from his lip and leant on the horn.

"There's forgiveness in my heart."

"And there's shit in your brains," Jon said. "She's a conniving cow, admittedly with nice tits. But still an evil bitch."

"I let her down."

"The only way you let her down was by not dying."

"Wanker!" Jon shouted suddenly, "May your bollocks shrink to currants."

"It's a woman," Ally said as a startled driver pulled sheepishly aside.

"May your pussy shrivel like a..." but Jon couldn't seem to come up with a comparable saying for the gender change.

Ally didn't think the Clio could take much more. It listed, something scraped the tarmac and the bearings smouldered. French engineering – stylish but lacking application to the task.

"Maggie said that I've changed and that she likes it. She says it's as if I've got in touch with my feminine side."

Jon cut the car back across two lanes of traffic, "If you were any more in touch with your feminine side, you'd be lactating."

Finally, Jon bumped the car up the curb and turned off the engine.

An unexpected stillness enveloped them as they sat staring straight ahead like a couple waiting for a roller-coaster just about to crest an incline. Ally had the urge to put his hands in the air.

"This it?"

A green and yellow neon cactus sign winked on and off.

"Look at the pretty lights," Alistair said.

"For the sweet love of our maker."

Opening the door, there was a rush of noise and movement, and it took Ally some moments to orientate himself. Gradually, the individual components began to separate: the middle-aged guitarist with a transvestite's over-rouged and sweaty cheeks perched on top of a cupboard, his fingers plucking away with little flicks; waiters sashaying between tables of divorced and desperate Shirley Valentines, packed together and howling, they'd abandoned their diets for the evening and looked hungry; empty bottles clanking in a plastic bin and glasses washed below the bar – the arms and shoulders of the barman moving briskly like a midwife impatient with a difficult birth; plumes of steam and the clatter of plates as food was dealt at the tables with a croupier's flourish.

Maggie was at the bar with her back to him and he had the impression she'd been there before. He took the stool next to her, but she didn't acknowledge him. A drink arrived which smelt of oranges. She was drinking in a self-absorbed way.

Food came and went without being touched. Time seemed to flow smoothly without interruption. He barely even noticed. Maggie's expression only changed when a waiter called Bepe passed.

"This is nice," Ally said, and suddenly she rose with the ferocity of a rescue buoy breaking the surface and headed to the toilets.

In the toilets, Maggie stared at her reflection. The mirror was pitted like an old X ray plate. It was as if a ghost was staring back at her – a cold, soulless thing. How pointless everything seemed. Maggie cursed herself for getting herself into this mess. Maybe she should just slip out the back and escape everything. But she also knew when you walked away from one thing, you were also walking towards the next, and there was no next for her. This was her last chance. Her hands were shaking as she dabbed her face with a piece of toilet roll, the feint scars on her wrists that neither Greg nor Ally had ever noticed glowed like thread worms under the skin.

Ally occupied himself watching a group of drunken students who were spilling drinks and talking loudly. At school, he'd briefly been on the outskirts of a gang that one day and without warning, had knotted like a flock of birds preparing to migrate and left him behind.

Maggie was resolute as she strode back to the table adjusting her dress. Even so, she had to order a sloe gin the second she saw his seal-pup face greeting her. It was like he was having the best evening of his life, and yet all she wanted to do was club him to death.

"There's a building in Ilford with a sign that says Monte Rose College and has a picture of a mortarboard on it," Ally said. "It's mostly foreigners who seem to file in and out."

Maggie thought if she didn't say anything he might just shut the hell up.

"Outside there are busts of Washington, Nelson Mandela and Winston Churchill on cement columns meant to look like stone."

Maggie couldn't help herself, "So?"

A pleasant hubbub was going around Ally like the popping of mud at a thermal spring. "Surely, they can't all have gone there."

Maggie gritted her teeth, how do people stand this sort of life?

"It's the building next to the driving test centre," Ally added.

He thought he would bring Jon here one day, on a weekday when it was less busy. Maybe they did half-price pensioner Thursdays like hairdressers did?

It took many more drinks to settle her nerves, but still, she didn't feel remotely drunk.

She sucked an ice cube and then crunched it, the pain it caused in her teeth was strangely reassuring. She shook the glass and the cubes clicked together. Maggie stuck out her tongue, the ice was dissolving on it becoming smooth and rounded. She withdrew it. She stuck it out again. Bepe smiled at her, a tea-towel slung over his shoulder.

"I haven't been out like this before," Ally said, but had nearly said 'we' meaning Jon and him.

"It's what people do."

"What people?"

"Normal people."

"Like us?"

"Like me."

Jon's opinion was that normality was overrated.

Bepe was moving effortlessly between the tables swaying his hips. Maggie thought he probably knew how to please a woman in bed.

"A woman needs a man who can take control," Maggie said under her breath. It was *cri de coeur*, she just couldn't help.

Ally didn't know where that came from or even if the utterance was meant for him. But he sensed that now was a moment when action was required. But what to do? Other men seemed to know instinctively how and when to act. Then before he knew what he was doing, he'd taken an ice cube from his untouched Ponche and dropped it down the back of her trousers.

Instantly, she was screaming at him, "Do you think I want something wet in my fucking pants? It's bad enough having you trying to fumble around my pussy like an old man looking for change in his purse."

The bar fell silent and Bepe headed over, slicing the tea towel either side of him like an explorer clearing the undergrowth. Everyone stared as Bepe took him by the scruff of the neck and marched him out.

He waited for Maggie, but she never came.

***

Rebecca was driving and they were doing 30mph. Sarge leaned forward and turned the siren on. She looked at him. There were wipes, wooden stirrers and tubes of sugar trodden into the carpet. An inexorable sluffage accompanied life and it was impossible to stop. Sarge knew this to a scientific certainty, it was thermodynamics and there were laws for this too.

The car came slowly to a halt and Rebecca yanked on the handbrake like she was breaking the neck of an injured creature. They weren't even on the slightest incline, yet Sarge knew he would need both hands to get it off.

Rain was coming down with a whoosh of arrows and Sarge imagined the people sheltering under umbrellas were soldiers with shields in a siege. They were outside Jon's flat on the unofficial stakeout that Rebecca had allocated their free time to. Everything was different in the dark, Sarge thought, as he peered into the gloom. Trees that were perfectly normal in the day now looked like the silhouettes of giant squid plunging down to the deepest water, and the weak light that seeped from the curtains at the flat window reminded Sarge of piss on the floor of a public urinal.

***

Jon was up when he got in, "How was it?"

"Nice."

"This guy here is making a Rouillard but he's screwed it up."

"Is this the episode from Stevenage?"

The aquarium light and gentle burble lulled Ally into a deep sleep. He woke with a start and although it felt as if he'd only slept for a matter of minutes, it could have easily been hours or even days.

Ally had dreamt he was in a hospital like a ferry terminal or MOT test centre, with plastic seating fixed to the floor and a Nescafe machine. Ally hated hospitals but for Fran they had been part of her everyday life. A lady was mopping the floor with long melancholic strokes as if in tune with the misery and fear that seeped from the new arrivals. They flowed from the front entrance and formed tributaries to the various wards. The doors opened and closed with a soft pneumatic sigh that never seemed to stop. Yet a lucky few headed in the other direction, handing out boxes of Quality Street to the nurses as if after a minor bingo win.

That was all he could recall, it had been years since he dreamt of Fran and he wondered why he would now. Jon was much as before, his outline occasionally lit by the TV as if by paparazzi that couldn't get enough of the wasted figure picking his toenails and with legs as bendy as a baby's. Looking back, these had been some of the best times with Fran – she emerging from another close call with death, wrapped in a blue blanket and looking sheepish. He recalled the hologram lady at the desk at St Barts, who encouraged everyone to use antibacterial gel with the cheerful detachment of an air hostess pointing out the escape routes. Fran used to wave goodbye to her as if to say, '*until next time.*'

Chapter 6

Last night Sarge'd visited his brother and as usual they sat at the window watching the white girls go by. A group of four had run with little steps to catch a bus, their high heels clipping like the report from news-hack's typewriter. Their breasts had swung from side to side engaged in a joyous Hokey Cokey and Sarge had wanted to shout out 'Oi'!

Beyond the net curtains there was a mysterious and heavenly world that neither of them had been able to reach. Arshad was nearing in a similar world, and maybe the curtains would soon be opening for him.

Later, they'd watched a Bollywood film called *Sholay* which they'd seen many times before. Sarge would imagine himself the self-important hero, karate-chopping his way through the bad guys that fell like skittles. He had a dictator's moustache that was jet black and never moved and wore impractical cream flares. For no apparent reason, women would break into dance for him, their arms snaking upwards so you could see their tight stomachs.

Afterwards, they had sat in silence. It had been a year since his brother could speak, although his mum said they talked as she made them tea. Sarge got nothing back but the stare. Once a week they did this.

Sarge was telling Rebecca about his evening.

"Gabbar Singh is like a chubby James Bond in a polyester suit, and the fighting is more Inspector Clouseau than trained assassin."

The speedometer dial glowed red and blue in the dark of the car. He couldn't tell if Rebecca was listening or even awake. But it didn't matter, he imagined himself to be single-handedly crossing a vast ocean with the night sky spread over everything as wonderful as a wizard's cloak. How peaceful that would be, the sea lapping at the hull as if moving a boiled sweet from cheek to cheek.

"Then, halfway through, the screen suddenly goes blank and the 'no input signal' comes up. We sit there looking at it and there's this momentary panic in my brother's eyes. Like this is it, death reaching out from the telly. And as if being dead might not be honey and virgins but rather background static and the late-night loneliness of all the channels being off air."

"They never go off air. Not now. Not for years," Rebecca said. "How old are you anyway?"

***

"You'll never believe what Cabbage Head goes and does now," Maggie was pacing back and forth.

"Cabbage Head?"

"He grabs one of the ice cubes from my drink, puts his fingers right in and picks it out, then he's sucking it with this big stupid grin on his face. Then, for fuck's sake, he tries to rub it over me like in some porno movie."

"No."

"Right there in front of everyone. Tries to rub it over my tits and fanny. The waiters were watching, everyone stopped and stared."

"What did you do?" Greg was intent. He was listening now.

"What the fuck do you think I did? I screamed and Bepe came over and sorted it."

"Bepe?"

But Maggie wasn't done yet.

"I swear to God, I want him dead. To crush up painkillers and put them in his baby food and kill once and for all the little fucker. Did you know he blends everything? If it doesn't go through a straw, it won't get in him." Flecks of spittle flew from her mouth, "Sod the getting him locked up for murder, I want him to knot in agony in front of me."

There is a picture on the wall of a bar in Crackow called The Chimera. Painted entirely in grey, people stare out of a tiny island they barely fit on. There are men with beards who look like the captains of ships that had been lost with all souls, charladies with child-killer hands wring scraps of sail, and a shrivelled hag cradles a baby whose head is too big. And as if things couldn't get any worse, in the background, dark storm clouds are gathering. Greg had seen this when he'd collected newspaper vouchers for a month solid thus entitling him to a weekend away for £5. The coach had been full of over-weight men with their over-talkative wives, and the journey was excruciating. Once there he'd ducked down into a beer cellar at random to come face-to-face with this nightmarish image. Now he could feel himself being painstakingly squeezed onto this island, yet another figure condemned to forever keep the company of the damned.

Chapter 7

It'd been another endlessly dreary shift and Sarge was at his locker when the call came. He decided against changing out of uniform even though it hadn't ever added to his authority as it did for others. Rather, it gave him the air of a museum curator looking round for a chair. He closed the door on his upturned trainers and jeans and left without feeling much at all. It could've been just another job, a bit of reluctant overtime he couldn't turn down.

As he entered the front door, his relatives stepped aside and stared at their feet. Sarge took off his shoes and went through to the lounge as he had many times before, but this time it was different. The most shocking thing was his mother's total collapse. He hadn't imagined it would be so devastating for her. He'd expected relief. Arshad was in the reclining chair while his mother wailed and fought his aunts who held her back with a wiry strength.

Upon seeing Sarge, she broke free and flung herself at him screaming, "Do something, do something!" Sarge was immobile and slowly she sank to her knees to rub Arshad's face. Sarge twisted his hat in his hands. At first, he couldn't work out what she'd wanted of him but gradually the full horror dawned on him. She wanted him to give Arshad the kiss of life. Sarge regretted the uniform now, he remembered how people expected things because of it: first aid, mediation, pet rescues, tourist information and even taxi rides. A uniform meant omnipotent powers.

Suddenly, she grabbed him by the jacket and pulled him closer. Sarge looked around wildly for help, but his cousins just smirked and the aunties hurried to the kitchen. Arshad's face loomed in front of him. It was obvious he was dead and had been for some time. It had the calm quality of a carved effigy, he was a fallen totem pole the villagers had gathered around to lift back into position.

His mum wailed without let up and her tears fell on the impassive face. The strong fingers pulled Sarge closer. He knew the drowning would take you with them given half a chance, it was the same with the dying. But there was no freeing himself from the weight of his mother hanging from his jacket. The room fell silent as his lips brushed against Arshad's. He could smell the internal rot that had set in years ago and nausea welled up in him, inching up his throat in bilge-pump lurches.

Unable to stand it a moment longer, he lurched toward the door pushing people aside, and for a ghastly moment his mum was dragged along like a hit-and-run victim. On the stairs, he tripped and banged his knee, but still he blindly fled the human debris and catcalls. When he reached the sanctuary of the bathroom, he slammed door and fell to the floor. Pressing his cheek to the cool enamel of the toilet, he cried. Sarge had never kissed another human being before on the lips.

He couldn't tell how much time had passed, but at one point, someone had knocked at the door. Sarge'd stifled his sobs with his fist and listened. Nothing.

Then a fist had thudded into the door and a voice hissed, "You useless sap." Then the footsteps had retreated. When he eventually returned, Uncle Mo had taken charge and decided Arshad should be carried to the bed that had been set up in the dining room. There was a makeshift way they handled the body. Men in parkas, carrying a dead person in the same coat they went to the Cash and Carry in. Sarge took a leg too, but no one asked him any questions now. It was hard and huge. He couldn't imagine the pain his brother had been in. And he'd never let on, grateful just for a drive up and down to the high road or to sit at the window watching the girls.

From the kitchen came the hubbub and aroma of cooking.

***

Greg was going over the plan yet again. If Fran was right and Ally had both life insurance and a will, then there were lots of possibilities. First the will; Cabbage Head had no family – he was an only child (as was Maggie) and his parents were dead. In fact, the more Greg thought about it, the more they had in common. Like peas in a misshapen pod.

So, the flat would go to Fran or Maggie. Either way he had it covered. So long as Maggie didn't find out about him and Fran. After all, she could be as mean as a rattlesnake on crystal meth when riled. And unless Fran was stringing him along, hoping he would get rid of Ally for her? Not likely, as she never planned anything, and how could she know what he and Maggie had in mind? Save some primal intuition that had survived the years of coke and smack abuse and occasionally lit up like a sprinkling of phosphorous in her cerebellum.

Besides, Maggie was certain Ally'd changed the will so she was the sole beneficiary; however, there was no way to be sure she had actually seen the documentation or probably Cabbage Head had just told her this. Even if the will went the way of Maggie and any life insurance to Fran, he was still good. Greg reckoned no matter what, so long he kept them both sweet (and apart), he would be fine and dandy.

Greg kicked back and took a hit of vodka… second, the insurance. Fran knew the payments had been kept up because she paid them. Through every breakdown, every spell of madness she'd paid, even if she had to suck some old man's limp cock to get the money. She'd told him this, using these words, and he'd had to fight down images from *Man versus food.*

The only problem he could see was that now a third element had come into play, and it was an added complication. This hadn't been part of the plan, but Maggie had improvised and taken the cards she'd been unexpectedly dealt and made a call. A murdered wife, for fuck's sake! A dead wife couldn't inherit nada. And worst of all, Ally in jail meant no payday from either angle, and all his hard work gone to waste.

Greg drank more, and his reasoning began to cloud. Everything had been simple before, but now it required some rejigging. Think, think, think. Once he'd seen a man at a bus stop dressed in full pirate gear with gators and a musket over his shoulder, he was bent over stuffing a loaf of Hovis 50/50 into a shopping trolley. Think.

No, getting Ally certified or sent to jail was not an option. Somehow, he had to die so that Fran or Maggie, or both, would inherit. And the first attempt had been such a cock up. Greg with his shoulders hunched in the crowd jostling Ally, Maggie surreptitiously squeezing his balls and winking in the scrum, and this enough to put him off, not managing as firm a purchase and shove as he'd intended.

But what now? Greg drank. He'd dispensed with the glass some time ago and was swigging from the bottle. Maybe, just maybe, things weren't so bad. Fran disappearing for a while might help in the short term by putting pressure on Ally. He was as serene and immortal as Kung Fu Panda, but maybe with the police on his case, it would precipitate some sort of crisis. All he had to do was keep Fran out of sight for a while and convince the police Ally had killed her, then see what happened. With any luck, Ally might even end up stepping under a bus himself, and at that, Greg roared, causing vodka to come back through his nose.

He was suddenly coughing and puking all in one, and for a moment struggled for air. As he wiped his mouth on his shirt and with his breathing returning to its regular rhythm, he was all too aware, in a visceral way, how quickly fortunes can change.

Although this scenario would ruin the life insurance, the will would still be valid. Fran could then pop back up and say hey, what's all the fuss about? If she got the flat, they would split it. Or maybe Greg could get Fran to make a will leaving everything to him and who knows, she could easily disappear again. With a lifestyle like hers, who would be surprised?

Greg nodded to himself, it was a solid plan. A patched-up one, but a plan, nonetheless. The next step was to get Fran out of the way and Maggie to keep on at the police – saying she didn't feel safe with a murderer at large and what the hell were they doing about it? He put the bottle to his lips but it was empty. That's when everything seemed to get muddled again.

***

Sarge waited in the hall as the Imam finished the prayers and padded past in his slippers.

Somehow, during the mayhem, the neatly paired shoes had piled up like Scalextric cars come off at the corners. He'd cleaned himself up as best he could but there were still a couple of gravy-like stains on his collar that had an acidic smell. A battered Ford Transit shuddered to a halt outside amid a cloud of mink-coloured smoke. Arshad's last journey would be in a van that on other days carried sides of lamb on hooks. His cousins shuffled out in small groups, some looking as if they were about to offer him a tip.

No one noticed Sarge drift off the back as the untidy procession made its way to the Mosque, and at Paula's café, he nursed a cup of milky tea. The scene was as depressing and ordinary as the funeral. The only other customer was a workman in a luminous tabard who read *The Daily Star* using his finger to trace each letter as if it were an illuminated manuscript. Bits of mashed up egg and chips occasionally fell from his mouth. It was the same sad and wasteful feeling Sarge'd had the one and only time he had bunked off school. The long, empty hours that had to be killed.

After managing only a few sips of tea, Sarge made his way to the Garden of Peace cemetery and re-joined his group as anonymous as when he'd left. They were in a queue. When one burial finished, another was waiting. Business was brisk. Men shuffled their feet and kicked the ground. A few huddled together making deals under their breath.

Sarge was surprised how wide ranging the group was. There were Christians, a pair of identical Maltese sisters in black veils, and a tall thin Sikh man who stood apart from everyone else. His brother had a secret scope to his life he could only wonder at. Most of the relatives had never come to see Arshad when he was alive.

Rain began to fall, and they huddled together dispiritedly under golf umbrellas supplied by the cemetery. It was like the early morning tee-off to a competition no one was particularly interested in. His mum was surrounded by the same aunties who had forced her into an unwanted marriage; they were watching the proceedings from across the road. In a couple of months, the graves would be cemented over. Tarmacking the dead was what happened to every man, woman and child alike; it was a parking bay that once reversed into, no one ever left.

Finally, it was their turn and they set off without a word, heading towards the digger as if some collective herd instinct had suddenly kicked in. The regularly spaced and uniform mounds were as even as tractor tread across a field. There was an anonymity in death that Sarge welcomed. At least there, he would be like everyone else. They stopped at a freshly dug hole that must be Arshad's. It looked little more than a small and unregulated building project, maybe for a greenhouse or ornamental pond. The rain gained energy now and then brushing his face like wet hair.

Sarge could see Naasima with his mum. She had green eyes and Sarge had admired his cousin from afar even though she never acknowledged him. Laughing with Bilal, sometimes her body would bend towards his and sometimes touch. Her and Rebecca could both be relaxed and natural with other men.

Then without ceremony, the coffin was unloaded and lowered into the ground and the whole process seemed to be over almost as soon as it had begun. Deals were finalised and sealed with a handshake. Uncle Mo picked clay off his shoe, muttering something under his breath, and the digger jerked into life and started filling in the hole.

Only then were the women allowed over, and they ran led by his mother. Grief-stricken, she had to be held back from throwing herself headlong into the grave. Clouds of diesel fumes belched from the digger and the operator worked his hands back and forth. Soon enough, the driver was skilfully tapping down the dirt with the digger's arm and Sarge was struck by the poignancy of this last act, like a giant ape gently kneading the ground with its knuckles.

As the crowd drifted away, Sarge was left alone with the raindrops that clung to the edge of his umbrella waiting for the first to let go. After which, the rest quickly followed. This happened over and over again. He was transfixed by this process that seemed to run around the edge of the umbrella in a never-ending process.

Eventually, he was snapped out of this reverie by his name being called, and he trudged over to Uncle Mo's Toyota. As they pulled away, slowly riding the speed humps, his mum kept staring out of the window as if it was all a terrible mistake. That Arshad might, any minute now, start clawing his way out and she needed to be there to help.

Turning into Romford Rd, they passed the newly arriving funeral parties who had the sombre and futile mood of savers queuing outside a collapsed bank.

"So fortunate to die on a Friday and in Ramadan too," Uncle Mo said. "Some people have all the luck."

Sarge watched the tears run down his mum's face like candle wax, and he wondered if she knew how lucky she was.

***

Jon's right arm hadn't grown properly, and Ally was still fascinated and repelled by it even after all these years. It was like a red balloon that hadn't fully inflated.

"There was this article in the Walthamstow Gazette today about a homeless ex-soldier," Jon said, "who kept a suit rolled up in his rucksack. He kept it just in case he got an interview. He'd carried it around for years. In the photo, he was holding it up."

There were only three fingers on his mutant hand and the middle one was much longer than the others. Maybe twice as long and when he smoked, the butt between the scaly digits was like a clenched turkey foot pulled smouldering from the oven.

"He was standing to attention with this sleeping bag over his shoulder like one of the wounded."

Ally could picture it.

"The thing was though, that I got the poor sod. The nights spent in piss-stained doorways, the fights and soup kitchen handouts. I got the suit thing. The hope of regaining some self-respect."

Ally wondered if Jon could have some sort of mechanical, prosthetic hand. A pale milky thing with the skin of an axolotl. He still wouldn't have wanted to touch it though. Or be touched by it.

"Everyone has something from before."

Jon had a Silvine notepad of poems, it was bright red with a spring down the spine and lined pages.

"The suit must be out of fashion by now," Ally said.

Chapter 8

'Take him out, be nice,' that's what Greg had said. It was alright for him, getting pissed and not painting. It had been years since she'd been impressed by his tortured artist routine, by the canvases stacked against the walls and the heady mix of anarchy and paint fumes. The studio had once represented all that was dangerous and different from her suburban upbringing. She'd been a late-in-life accident that her parents hadn't the energy or interest for. It was the excitement she craved when she let him have her for the first time on the milking stool all those years ago. But it hadn't been long before poverty and routine had set in. The drinking getting heavier, the progress less, the squalor sticking to her hands like a smell that couldn't ever wash off. And then he started taking out his failure on her, the rages and beatings.

Maggie said, "Let's go for a drive."

"I didn't know you had a car?"

"I borrowed it."

"Have you got a license?"

"Do you want to fucking go or not?"

They headed east along the A12 and the winter sun was candlewax pressed between the trees and it barcoded the road. Ally could almost hear the pings as they sped along.

Despite the fly-tipped fridges, scorched mattresses and sofas, Ally was full of good cheer. The discarded furniture was better than that at Jon's flat. Black bin-bags spilled powdery residue that clumped like old ladies' hair and the dirt-choked nettles swayed merrily as they passed by. Ally stared at these things as if they were wonders of the world.

After an hour or so, they entered Frinton. There was a school, Brenda's hair salon, bungalows and estate agents, none of which appeared to be open. It was only 4 o'clock and it was already getting dark. Maggie followed the signs to the beach and they parked by a concrete wall. The streetlamps seemed to come on reluctantly one by one, as if they too could hardly stand the place. The sea moved in a slack and sickening way like a drunk trying to get to his feet and each time failing.

Maggie's mobile peeped and she started typing with her thumbs.

"There are beach huts further down," Ally said. "Apparently they're on stilts and you can stay the night, but you're not supposed to."

Beep beep.

The screen glowed blue and she smiled as her thumbs danced over the keys. The rain became heavier and more persistent. With its back bent by the wind, it tapped its way along the walkway like blind man with a cane.

Ally thought of his mother. She had died a long time ago but he still missed her. Somehow, he always thought that those times might return, and he would be holding her hand again amid the Saturday shoppers, overcoats brushing his face and a moving forest of thighs. Frinton was a place that made you feel close to the dead.

"I'm hungry," Maggie announced, and without waiting for a response, she started the car. They reversed out and after negotiating poorly lit streets they ended up an industrial park on the outskirts of town. The golden arches shone brightly above the carpark.

"I'm addicted to the coffee here," Maggie said. "I collect the tokens, look."

He could see several cards in her purse. She pulled one out before snapping the purse shut.

"Are we going in?"

"Drive-thru."

They pulled up to the kiosk.

"What will you have? I'm paying," Maggie said.

"I want to see the menu."

Ally chewed his Chicken McSandwich slowly; nothing moved on the empty tarmac square which the units faced. A harsh, fluorescent light flared from the Travel Lodge as from an abattoir's freezer. The automatic doors hushed open and a couple in their office clothes came out. They looked gloomily around, turned up their collars and with a brief touch of fingers, they parted, going their separate ways with the determination of salmon. Ally couldn't imagine anything good or exciting happening in a Travel Lodge in Frinton.

At ten o'clock, Maggie dropped him home; it was his birthday and Ally was 46 years old. As he climbed the stairs to Jon's flat, he reflected that the coffee hadn't been anything special.

***

The men were in the lounge and the women in the kitchen as Bilal came in bow-legged and languid, all smiles and handshakes. He caused quite a stir and Sarge had heard talk that he boxed a bit. Even Rebecca had turned up in a Burberry headscarf. She'd come with a couple of male colleagues he couldn't remember the names of. Sarge guessed they were middle-ranking CID as he'd only ever seen them in uniform at functions. Only the very top and very bottom wore uniforms in the police. Like surgeons being called Mr, it was a reverse snobbery.

They shook his hand and said they were representing the station. One called him Simon. Sarge thanked them for coming and brought them samosas. They stood awkwardly with Sarge at a loss what to say, even in his own house he was the unwanted guest.

Backing away unnoticed, he seemed to merge with the rubber plant in the corner where he wasn't in the way. From his hiding place, he watched as it slowly dawned on them they would have to sit on the floor. They exchanged looks like missionaries coming across a tribe of small, naked people. Then the slightly older, plumper one took control, circling in a discontent way, he chose a spot at random, and down he went; onto one knee and then keeling sideways, hitting the floor his legs akimbo, and bulging slacks stretched tightly to clearly show a pair of low-hanging bollocks. But through all this, his plate remained held aloft like a pub darts trophy after an intoxicated win. Soon enough, they were both stuffing their faces, and Sarge was appalled anew how white people ate with such ferocity.

When Sarge was young, there had been a cement bullfrog in the garden, and it'd had an idiotic red tongue hanging out. He had no idea where it had come from as the garden was paved over and unused. His dad hadn't ever ventured beyond the patio doors which were like an impenetrable forcefield to him. Probably the previous residents had left it. Through his childhood it had sat there mostly ignored, like Sarge himself. He had felt a kinship with it and now he wondered if it was still there, impassive to the surrounding misery and still licking its face.

Slipping away to the kitchen with an empty tray tucked under his arm, Sarge found Bilal sitting at the table. Everyone was laughing, including Rebecca. Usually only the women, children and disabled were allowed in the kitchen. They fell silent when they noticed him at the door. No one invited him in. As he retreated, the voices started up at his back like an interrupted waterfall.

Sarge envied Bilal's confidence and swagger even though he worked at the self-service tills in Tesco's. Back in the lounge, he sat in the only space left. It took him a while to realise he was next to his father. It was as if Sarge was having trouble remembering how this man fitted into his life. Every day he'd disappear off to work before they got up and then in the evenings, he'd lie on the sofa in the kitchen watching the big TV. The rest of them were usually in the lounge watching Coronation St. His father had been little more than an extra cushion on the sofa.

Uncle Mahmood came over and shook his father's hand. He was tall with a fine beard, and his father's small hand disappeared into Uncle's overpowering grip. Many years ago, Arshad had turned up at Uncle's uninvited and been brought back immediately. There had been harsh words between his mum and uncle at the front door. They had never visited again.

When Uncle Mahmood had left, his father said, "I passed blood this morning."

Sarge nodded. His dad retained a heavy accent even after decades in the country.

"From my balls."

Sarge said nothing.

"From my balls… You understand?"

Sarge gritted his teeth, "Yes, Father."

And that seemed to be it. The father/son time, the words of wisdom in this time of mourning. Sarge was all too aware of the chilling medical complications that awaited him also. There would be shame followed by the inevitable tidying away of an inconvenient life.

"The other day, I fell over on the way to the factory," his father unexpectedly added. "I still went to work."

Sarge thought everyone needed to belong.

It was only later that Sarge realised his father had been saying *bowels,* but this provided little comfort.

***

Ally was going over his date with Maggie – it was the second since the accident which he looked upon as year zero, where everything was reset. As he spoke, Jon's malformed forefinger impatiently picked at the chair arm, loosening a thread and then tugging at it. Ally concluded that overall, he thought it had gone well. They then both watched the finger for a while as if neither of them had control of it.

Then Jon said, "I had someone once, Mary."
Ally pricked up his ears sensing this might be
important. Something from Jon's past, the years
when their lives had been separate. "Mary was a
dental nurse which means she had the uniform but
not the qualifications. Neither of us had anyone so
we just sort of fell in together." Like he and Jon had
now, Ally thought. If not for a chance bumping into
each other at the Turkish grocers when Ally had got
off the wrong tube stop, he wouldn't be where he
was now. "My only relative was a mad aunt in
Worthing I visited at Christmas and slept on the
floor. We were both glad when I stopped going. She
was probably glad when she died too, I know I
was."

Ally hadn't known Jon to ever have a
girlfriend. At school, there had been rumours that
Jon's mum had killed herself in the bath, which
gave him a sort of unapproachable aura like a
Plymouth Brethren.

"One day, Mary tells me she's met a Greek waiter and leaves. Two months later, she's back. He's cheated on her, not once but every opportunity he gets. Then she goes again and this time it's a painter and decorator from Rochester. Then she's back and this time pregnant. The painter and decorator gets a brain tumour and can't work, he's having surgery and has nowhere to live. So, he moves in as well. Both of them in my flat. They in the bedroom and me the sofa. I must've been as fucking soft in the head back then as you are now." Ally knows this is Jon giving him something that he's never given him before or likely would ever would again. Advice.

"She has the kid, and tumour-guy has surgery but loses the sight in his good eye. He's practically blind and can't work, and they all in my bedroom. The council drags its feet, the kid gets sick and the three of us wait up five nights in a row at St Georges. The blind guy stumbling about, Mary in bits, but the kid pulls through. Then a house comes up across town and they move out." Jon put his good hand down the front of his jogging bottoms and rearranged everything with the well-practised action of a butcher setting out his window display. "By now I'm used to the sofa and stay there. That's how I got into Come Dine."

Ally now slept in the bedroom of the blind painter and cheating wife, as the TV silently flickered day and night like subterranean pipe-welding.

Chapter 9

Sarge was parked up outside the flat. He was staking out the place now in his own time. Since his brother's death, it was the only thing he could think to do. He was hunkered down in a hoodie and jeans. Like all policemen, he tended to dress too young when not on duty. Sarge could picture Zippie and Bungle in the warm flat, drinking beer and watching porn.

He gripped the wheel and his knuckles whitened – how easy it was to momentarily imagine himself part of the life that passed all around him. White people didn't feel pain like everyone else; in fact, they didn't feel full stop. They were bloodless, cold and mean. But no matter how hard he pressed when his strength failed, his own skin tone seeped back. No, you couldn't ever escape who you really were. And Alistair Duncan was a murderer who hadn't the right to have a fit girlfriend when Arshad

had just been buried with less care than a re-potted houseplant.

***

It had been impossible for Ally to get out of his head the soldier more frightened of a camera than any enemy gun. It was the sort of newspaper cutting discarded without a second glance by council workmen, sent to clear a flat when the smell got too much for the neighbours.

"Did you write anything today?" Ally asked.

Jon put down his bowl of Cheerios, wiped the milk that was beading in his beard and reached for his notebook.

"At school there was always someone with a built-up shoe," Jon said, "but mostly at primary, not so much at secondary. Something must happen to them between the two. A sort of culling. Also, an unnaturally blond girl with blue National Health glasses. You don't tend to see them much now either."

And someone with a spastic arm, Ally thought to himself. Probably Jon didn't notice this kid because it was himself.

"Is the poem about a child with a built-up shoe?" Ally asked.

Jon squinted at the notebook and cleared his throat.

"It's called, *Every village has a Goth.*"

Ally closed his eyes.

Every village has a Goth,
A Goth and a goat-lady.
Every village has a wife-beater
And a swindler-solicitor.
Every village has a shut-in
Who watches the children go by.
And every village has a murder,
The body kept in a freezer.
Sandra's Salon shut indefinitely

And no more said.

"A love poem?" Ally said.

Chapter 10

His tongue rolled like a poisoned dolphin washed by the tide. As Greg slowly emerged into consciousness, the room swayed like the scenery in a low budget sci fi programme. Never again. That was it, even the thought of drinking made his stomach lurch. He'd slept in his clothes and his groin felt warm and musty. He swung his legs off the sofa and let everything stabilise before attempting the next big move. As he stood, his belly swung sickeningly as an overfilled bucket of slop would. It was degrading being a drunk and degrading being old, but together was more than even he could bear.

Greg padded to the kitchen, put the coffee on and then went for a piss. As the steam rose, he went over the situation again and was sure, after Maggie's improvisation, he had to get Fran disappeared pronto.

His piss was rancid; the colour of tobacco and smelt of kippers. It was amazing that something so toxic could be in him without killing him. He shivered to think what else might be brewing away in there. His guts were probably like the mountains of Mordor with lava flows indeterminate, oozing black stuff ready to pollute the world.

When the coffee was ready, he took it through to Fran. Her face was scrunched up where she'd slept on it. Greg wondered if she'd had a stroke. Who said it was only Maggie who was putting in the hard shifts? He left the cup and took his mobile back to the kitchen where he scrolled down and rang.

"Time to up the ante. Tell the police he's been acting weird; well, weirder than normal. Say you don't feel safe and maybe you're next on his hit list, ask for updates on what they're doing. Play the frightened rabbit."

Greg thought he could hear her snort.

"But she could turn up any time," Maggie said.

"Leave that to me."

There was a long silence.

"I've told you nothing seems to rile him, he's all Placido Domingo."

"Well just fucking try," he said cutting her off.

In the bedroom, Fran was sipping coffee.

Greg smiled, "Let's go away, baby, just me and you."

"Where?"

"Paris." Greg thought he'd kill two birds with one stone, look at the rental market, where to stay... Just kind of sus things out.

"Ok," she said over the rim of the cup.

"Do you like butter?"

"Margarine."

***

It'd been a long day of domestic disputes, scooters terrorising the pavements and pulling over cars with faulty brake lights or personalised number plates like N1XXi or S3RG1Z. Sarge had wearily listened to the complaints and threats of owners of pink Fiat 500s or white Mercedes as he wrote them up, whilst all the time in his head the line from a song went around and around, *A man must indeed be small to write his name on a piss house wall.*

Their underpowered Ford car reeked of burger fat and cappuccino. It'd been decent of Rebecca to come to the funeral, though he still couldn't figure how she knew. Probably DC Barnet, his CO, had told her. Rebecca was always sprawling over his desk, and Sarge was having difficulty keeping his eyes off her as her skirt rode up revealing the top of her stockings.

She was drifting in and out of sleep occasionally making snuffling noises, and her hair was fanning over the headrest.

Outside, it was a desolate scene: a young mother struggled with a three-wheel buggy as she negotiated between dog crap, squashed fruit, broken crates from the market and looted bags of clothing spewing from the charity shop doors.

In the car, it was stuffy, and Rebecca's shirt was stretched tight at the buttons reminding Sarge of tied-off balloons. A black bra clearly visible and the milky skin of her breasts was overbrimming the cups as she breathed. He felt his cock stir. Oh fuck, she was teasing him. Her legs fell open a little wider and the skirt inched up higher. Sarge thrust his hand between his knees and held them tight as he rocked back and forth. Was she really asleep? Even the night seemed to hold its breath as if to see what would happen next.

The rain had stopped now, and it left an empty feeling in Sarge like an adventurous relative leaving for far flung places. He had never touched a white woman, had barely touched any woman at all. It was forbidden fruit. Rebecca moaned and readjusted her ass, he could see her thighs now. They looked moist and he wanted to put his hand between them. Sarge had seen Rebecca fool around with the lads in the canteen, she would grab their groins and do a comic juggling routine with her tits as they whistled and catcalled. Sarge didn't think she respected herself. But if she was like that with them, surely, she would be just as easy with him if only he could lighten up.

In Sarge, the disease moved slower, but still it moved. As inevitable and remorseless as geology. At night, he could feel it wake, his disease was his only companion. He would show her he could joke. Asians were funny too, weren't they? And sometimes intentionally so. Who was that fat Asian guy? Something Djalili. But he was Iranian. A fat funny Iranian. Didn't he do Ayatollah jokes before al-Qaeda or Isis? He looked like a magic carpet salesman. Whatever happened to him? Maybe they caught up with him in the end.

Sarge's heart was racing. Surely, she wanted him to josh with her as others did. That's what she was telling him. He moved his hand forward, his brown fingers showed vividly against the bright white shirt. It was as if he was alive for the first time and his senses burned in him. He was Joan of Arc. His hand shook as he felt the taught nylon, but at the very moment of touching, he pulled it back. Forcing his hands between his knees again he rocked. What the hell was he thinking of? It was professional suicide. Molesting a work colleague. He'd be sacked and bring even more disgrace on his family.

Rebecca sighed and the dough rose, spilling over the black cups only to gently subsided again. Her legs shifted and he could see the gusset of her black pants. They reminded him of PE classes and his first contact with girls; the shrill squeals and acrid smell of plimsoles came back to him.

The lights from the all-night chemist and pizza booth reflected a cheapskate Mardi Gras in the oily pools that patched the road. There was madness in the air. Sarge had never been drunk or even tasted alcohol, but this must be what it was like – the urge to abandon all responsibility, giddiness and the impulse to live for the moment.

His brother's lingering death and the emptiness was ever present with him, and for once, Sarge wanted warmth, laughter and the embrace of another human being. Blood pounded in his temples and, as the lights from the streetlamps and shop windows spun and stopped with a juddering halt at Jackpot, he lunged forward. Suddenly, his hand was stuck in her blouse with the material stretched round it like a vet's plump hand deep in a cow's privates. Rebecca was awake now and thrashing away, her legs and arms rotated furiously, and she caught him square across the face.

With repeated tugging, he managed to work his hand free and shrunk back as far from her as he could. His knee had somehow wedged against the horn, and he covered his face. He wanted to be anywhere but there.

Rebecca was swearing and shouting and even with the endless blare of the horn, he could clearly hear the words full of contempt, "You dirty bastard, I would never fuck you!"

In his head and wanting it all to stop and to be home in bed, he said, "But you would everyone else.'

***

Greg was already angry when he got home to find his front door wide open. Maggie didn't seem to be getting anywhere and he'd begun to wonder if her heart was really in it. In fact, he doubted if anyone was as committed to the project as him. That's why when he cautiously entered the flat to find Fran slumped in a duvet and blood up the wall, he took it as no more than how his luck was going at present. He even wondered if somehow, he had crossed into a parallel universe where things were even more shit for him than they were in his one. Fran appeared almost see-through and although her eyes followed him, they conveyed nothing. No pleading, no regret, no anger. Pale and insipid, they swayed with his weak gravitational pull as he stepped over her and into the kitchen.

This wasn't in the plan, none of it was. Why was everyone trying to screw him over? He poured himself a vodka and knocked it back. He looked at Fran. The eyes reminded Greg of something par-boiled and beginning to set in its own transparent jelly. Wincing, he took another shot. These bloody women were giving him an ulcer for sure… and those fucking eyes never even blinked or looked away. Not in any moment of feigned tenderness had he ever looked so long into them. Greg took another hit.

Though he needed her out of the way, he also needed her alive. She was 50% of his chance of the money. There seemed to be an awful lot of blood for such a small person, and where it soaked into the duvet, it was a darker red than that on the wall.

Greg picked up the phone and saw he had a text, he only just stopped himself from opening it. This time the vodka didn't burn so much. He stepped back over her and went downstairs to the street door. The air was clear and fresh and there was no one around. He took several deep breaths.

Seven was the dead time round here, a pause between the commuters heading home and the career drinkers with the red-tipped noses of a ventriloquist's dummy.

Reinvigorated, Greg bounded back up the stairs and, without pause, gathered her onto his shoulder. He was surprised to find this was no more trouble than handling a bag of compost. His feet seemed to dance back down the steps as if he were a compere in top hat and tails – under different circumstances, he might've even bounced a cane off the pavement to catch in mid-air. Instead, he placed her on a pile of bin bags that, he thought, looked rather comfy. No worse than the PVC bean bags they have in advertising agency canteens and special needs schools.

Greg couldn't look at the eyes any longer. No one passed. He waved his fingers at her before heading back in, taking the steps two at a time. In his mind, he was sure he fully intended to dial 999 when he swiped the phone, but the little yellow envelope caught his attention and Greg just couldn't help clicking on it.

Chapter 11

The day had rung clear, and the sky was a Madonna blue which planes had scored with an ice skater's graceful arcs. The silence was broken by a handful of pigeons occasionally snaping into muffled flight. Sarge was perched on a stool and trying to block everything out. When he opened his eyes, the events of the previous evening came flooding back like irresistible sunlight. His mum was reciting from the Holy Book. Hunched over on her stool, she was as round as the frog in their cement garden. She was praying so hard it was like she was tugging at a tree root that wouldn't budge.

The groundsman moved slowly but deliberately. He didn't seem to be in a hurry to do anything, least of all work. Every time Sarge glanced over to him, he seemed to catch his eye, at which point Sarge would look away. Then, as if he couldn't bare it any longer, the guy began shouting and gesticulating.

It took Sarge a moment or two to realise it was directed at him and his mum. Sarge kept his head down and his eyes shut. Mostly, it was aimed at his mum, saying she had no right to be there and should be at home. There seemed to be so much hate in him. The voice rose and fell but thankfully didn't come any closer. He heard his mum shuffle but didn't look.

Eventually, Sarge summoned up enough courage to peer through his lashes like a cat through the bars of its carry box. The danger was over, he'd turned away kicking a lump of clay as he went. Sarge should have stood up for his mum as a son and police officer, but he felt unequal to both roles. Since he was young, she'd been defying men: learning to drive (*who else was going to take my sons to their hospital appointments?*), being on the board of the TS charity, and having Christian friends. She had a courage and spirit that they deemed dangerous, and for the rest of her life, they'd made her pay.

***

It was two weeks before Fran turned up looking paler than a ghost in sunblock.

"Hey, hon, you look great," Greg said. "Let's take that trip we planned. I've packed my speedos."

She stood just inside the door as if apologising for still being alive.

"Paris isn't on the coast."

Greg made a big clownish gesture as if to say, 'what can you do?'

Neither mentioned the dumping in the street incident.

***

Unsurprisingly, Paris had been a disaster and now Greg turned his thoughts to Amsterdam, where they spoke English and in *Diamonds are Forever,* there was a pretty assassin who lived on a barge. Greg could almost feel the gentle pitch and roll as another boat chugged past. Red wine stains splotched across the table like an Aboriginal cave painting, a bicycle and herb patch on deck. That would be a life.

His doubts had begun even before they'd reached the check-in at Stansted. Among the confident and purposeful backpackers, Greg had suddenly realised he didn't have a clue what to do or where to go. As he made his disorientated way across the polished floor, even his suitcase-on-wheels seemed to be giving him a mocking round of applause.

At the weighing machine, he had frozen. There was a computer with big buttons for the elderly and a hole to push his luggage through but couldn't figure out what to do. Confident men with beards and ponytails tapped away at the screen without a pause in their animated conversations and were dispensed with the appropriate paperwork. The different languages seemed harsh and hostile and made him feel a long way from home. And he hadn't even left yet. He couldn't have felt more out of place if outlaws with cartridge bandoliers across their shoulders were pressing him for international fun in some fly-infested, swamp bar. Finally, Fran had taken his ticket and saved him with a few quick taps.

She knew exactly what to do, at ease with a madness no worse than the one in her head. He trailed behind her as she navigated through the chaos; she even spoke French to the man behind a counter. A bottle of cologne was confiscated from his hand luggage and security sniggered at him as if he were the idiot-son. Then he made the scanner beep and removed his belt and shoes. It went off again. Then a female guard frisked him like she was gutting a fish.

What surprised him most through the whole ordeal was Fran's serenity which he'd never seen before. She was normally hunched and fast moving as if expecting some sort of attack. He put it down to the garbled input being nothing new to her, and the airport finally being a reality matching her own internally generated scrambled messages. She managed all this whilst dragging a huge bag across the floor like culled livestock.

"What you got in the luggage, hon?"

She didn't answer.

From this low point, it got even worse. He subsumed all responsibility to her and was as helpless as the infirm. They stayed in a hotel where the room was a foot bigger than the bed. In the morning, a bowl of instant coffee and a baguette were left outside their door. They ate sitting on the mattress. At Montmartre, tourists in shower ponchos moved from one brightly coloured blanket to the next, inspecting the cheap jewellery and leather bracelets as watchful Africans pitched their wares in whispers. The only artist was painting a squirrel which was hunched over like a gnome with a fishing rod. But still the tourists huddled around admiringly. Greg thought he might as well have been in Eastbourne. Even the French girls weren't as pretty as he'd hoped; in fact, the boys and girls seemed wholesome and interchangeable like the youth wing of an evangelical sect.

Most of the time, they stayed in the room and watched TV. The only channel in English was CNN which they left running day and night. Eventually, it began to develop the malevolent presence and Greg increasingly wanted to smash it to pieces, but he feared the silence more. Fran took a range of pills following no discernible dosage or pattern. Even when they had managed to go out during the day and without attracting attention, he'd found the food expensive and nothing special. Everything came with chips. Chips like you got in takeaways. French fries, he supposed.

She wanted to visit the Latin Quarter and the evening they decided to go, she hauled her bag from the cupboard with both hands and over to the bathroom. Half an hour later, she came out wearing a moth-eaten fur coat that made it look as if she was in the process of being eaten by a mangy bear. Makeup peeled from her cheeks like marzipan and, God forbid, she appeared to be naked underneath. Greg swallowed in disbelief. She looked like a drag act under a harsh spotlight and with sluttish intent. They went out like that, arm in arm.

Even where no one knew them and the alternative crowd were out, they caused a stir. Mercifully, none of the restaurants let them in and Greg was relieved when the excruciating experience was over. The next day, Greg begged the receptionist to book a flight home as soon as possible. Jail, murder, torture, anything was better than this.

Chapter 12

Sarge tuned the radio to XFM just to annoy Rebecca. At work, he knew the lads called it Malcolm X FM. He turned it up loud and put on his sunglasses even though it was pitch black outside. Rebecca immediately switched it back to Magic and swayed along to a Billy Joel number. Secretly he thought less of people with conservative musical taste as he did those who chewed gum. For some reason, he thought that they lacked real-life experiences.

Rebecca was wearing the shapeless regulation trousers he'd never seen her in before. They accentuated her hips. Policewomen generally had sturdy hips and Sarge wondered if it was part of the entry requirements. A test behind closed doors, similar to the indignity boys went through at school when a doctor cupped their testicles and asked them to cough. He pictured strange medical pincers with curved ends and a circular scale at the fulcrum.

Empty Dixie takeaway boxes littered the street and they seemed to gather around the puddles like animals in a drought did. Men in vests peered out from steamy windows, and in turn they seemed to have the self-same boxes upturned on their heads at a jaunty angle. Sarge thought how his parents had travelled halfway round the world for this. It hardly seemed worth it.

Rebecca mostly ignored him now yet flirted even more vigorously with everyone else. Sometimes his colleagues would look over his way and laugh. Neither of them had spoken of that evening, and Sarge reckoned it was only that he knew her secrets, knew what a Thames Estuary racist she was, that stopped her filing an assault charge. She was ambitious and would climb over him in a heartbeat – one less ethnic minority was one less competition. But she was smart too and knew there was no need for an ugly HR incident.

He would be dead soon, or at least off long-term sick. It would be his turn for the wheelchair and to watch the people pass as the curtains reached out to him.

***

After Paris, Greg didn't care much about anything anymore. Why didn't he just get rid of Fran himself? He'd been stuck with her for weeks now and everyone already thought she was dead. It was only that there wasn't a body. That was easily solved, and all he'd have to do was plant some evidence in that cesspool of a flat to incriminate Duncan.

Then he'd get Maggie to waggle her tight ass at Sergeant Constable and sit back and wait. Duncan wouldn't be able to take all that pressure and maybe would even top himself. In that case, there wouldn't be any life insurance pay out, but what the hell? Maggie was certain the flat was left

to her, and waiting wasn't an option anymore.
Besides, she was beginning to look far too settled in
Duncan's flat.

When Greg'd called round last week, she'd
been cooking and even made him piss sitting down.
It had shocked him. She said it was because she had
just cleaned, but he knew it was the shape of things
to come. An emasculation of the spirit and body.
No, he had to act and finally be rid of the
bloodsucking leaches that clung to him.

Maggie had been unable to contain her
smugness as she held up the key to Jon's. Greg
didn't ask how she'd got it and she didn't say.
Later, he couldn't think what had possessed him to
make a Blu Tack impression of it, hunched at the
Formica table in his kitchen with a big grin.

And then he'd gone to the Timpson's kiosk
in Sainsbury's, handing the blue blob over like a kid
caught with a pornographic magazine. He'd vaguely
remembered that they employed ex-offenders and
he handed it over to the grizzly guy in a leather

apron. He winced even to think of it, his conspiratorial wink and guy looking at him as if he wanted to leap over the counter and tear him to pieces. He'd scrunched the ball and ran as the con had lifted the phone. Next time, he went to a cobbler's and just took the key.

* * *

The fairground ride went whoosh. It hissed and wheezed with blasts of pneumatic decompression like lorries breaking. Jon and Ally had their faces pressed up against the railings like Mexicans at the border. The dust rose up at the Muslim Fair. It had the slow human weight of the hajj on TV but with more fun. On the rides, the women shrieked as they fought their burkas.

"They drive like that too," Jon said.

Sarge made his way through the press with discomfort. The men reeked of cologne and the girls had filigree designs around their eyes. With faces as smooth as pebbles, they chatted away excitedly into phones that were tucked into headscarves. The human spirit will out, Sarge thought. Once or twice, he felt the shape of a slim body under the chador brush past him. Men in sharp suits and aviator sunglasses were making the girls turn away with mock outrage and giggle in huddles. Sarge was the only one on his own and the only one shaved.

At the shooting gallery, air pellets dinged the metal targets and someone Sarge had seen handing out leaflets at the Carphone Warehouse raised his arms aloft when he won a teddy. He cried out 'another dead Yankee' but no one cared. Sarge bought pink candy floss on a stick and headed home; his pleasures were the same as when he was a child.

Chapter 13

Greg drank two pints of Guinness in quick succession before heading off to B&Q. He'd wound through the canyons of shelving with a green basket and a pleasant buzz, who the hell could reach up that high? He selected a roll of duct tape, latex gloves, a Stanley knife and some plastic sheeting. Queuing at the checkout, he suddenly realised that his basket looked like an abductor's kit for beginners. Maybe the till staff were trained to look out for such things. He glanced at the fat and unenthusiastic teenager at the till and doubted it. However, he went back and got three rolls of wallpaper, a floppy brush and some paste.

When he'd got through security, there was the same minor triumph he'd felt when passing passport control unchallenged. He threw the wallpaper and paste in the bin, the brush he kept. Maybe he would go big for his next artistic period.

***

"I've got tickets for a concert," Jon said.

"A gig?"

"No, a concert with Lang Lang."

"The panda?"

"The pianist."

"A piano playing panda, cool."

"There's no fucking panda."

***

A black woolly hat was pulled down so as to
cover most of Greg's head, and the latex gloves
gave him the otherworldly hands that albinos have.
He felt like making the over-exaggerated
movements of a mime artist. In his pocket there was
a Tic Tac box with a pubic hair inside, which he'd
collected with the care of an entomologist from his
bed that morning. When Fran left, he found it,

holding it up to the light with a pair of tweezers like a tiny, silver spring.

It had taken ages for Laurel and Hardy to leave and when they had, it was almost arm in arm. One tall and thin, the other short and fat and struggling to keep up. Greg thought they should've been carrying a ladder and bucket between them. He couldn't imagine where they would be going together.

The key turned with a soft click and as he pushed open the door with his fingertips, jumped back. No siren went off and nothing blew up. Greg breathed a sigh of relief and tiptoed in. Ensuring the door was shut behind him, Greg waited for his eyes to grow accustomed to the dark. There was the desperate, last-gasp sound of a respirator like the heavy sucking of feet being constantly pulled from mud. But when his sight had adjusted, he found it was only the gurgling of a green and empty fish tank. All this sneaking around was making him paranoid.

A nicotine light seeped in from the streetlamps giving everything a preserved in formaldehyde feeling. The sofa was collapsed like that of an over-used prostitute who'd seen too many men in her life. It was like stepping back in time, not to a romantic past but to a turgid and hopeless one which people tried to forget. Greg pulled himself together. He had a job to do and didn't want to be there any longer than necessary, for he feared that something deep inside himself that was easily drawn to sleazy indolence.

The bathroom was no better; the lino lifted around the toilet, a Bic razor lay embedded in a bar of soap and the shower curtain hung like a toenail-coloured ghost in the corner. Quickly, he fumbled to open the Tic Tac box and lift the toilet seat in the same motion, the porcelain rim was so hairy it could've been wearing a mink stole. Greg gagged as he tore off some toilet paper, wiped round and flushed. With a flourish, he placed the hair in a prominent position. It looked like an unfurling bean sprout struggling for light. Greg lowered the seat carefully to protect it. Backing out of the room he was suddenly stopped in his tracks. A chipped mirror hung over the sink just like the one his parents had had, which impassively watched them all grow old. Greg had imagined it emitting an odourless gas that greyed the hair, folded the skin and doubled over everyone who looked it in the eye. When he'd cleared their small council flat, he'd smashed it with a brick.

Greg hurtled out the flat, snapping off his gloves as he went like some surgery for a despot had gone disastrously wrong and was now fleeing for his life.

When he got his breath back, Greg made the call, "Send the police round to the bunker now. I don't care how you do it, just do it. Say Brain Dead confessed, say he murdered her and chopped her up in the bath. Tell them to fucking hurry before the evidence is lost." He cut the line before Maggie could reply.

And then for no reason, and for the first time since childhood that wasn't an emergency, he began to run. Like joggers did, to see if it was fun. It must bring them something other than a premature heart attack, he reckoned. But he sensed his legs and arms weren't working smoothly, not how he intended. Greg felt too much rotation and his moobs swung from side to side.

It never occurred to him that the pubic hair could've been his.

***

Ally counted out the change from his purse with studied concentration and felt the impatience of the queue as he carefully tucked it into his pocket. They'd dressed up for the Barbican with Jon in his Motorhead T shirt and Ally his funeral suit. Carrying the coffees over to the tall tables usually found in student bars, Ally was reminded of Vera's robust poise. It was harder than it looked carrying drinks without significant spillage. He climbed aboard the stool with the apprehension of a man mounting an examination table in a paper gown.

Silently, they sipped from cardboard cups and watched the crowd gather. Jon had a thing for Chinese girls and once had admitted he went to concerts because it 'brought them out' and made it sound like an allergic reaction. Ally had to admit there were a lot there. Some wore thick glasses and even seemed to have western boyfriends. The Chinese guys looked serious and geeky.

"An industrious but short-sighted people," Jon said.

A queue was forming at the coffee bar and Ally was glad he'd gone up early. An old woman bent nearly in half was waiting her turn, she made a parting in the line like an ornament in the middle of a bookshelf. She had a stick and had to put an opposing crick in her neck to look ahead. Sad but kind eyes peered out from behind spectacles. A kindly tortoise. There must be difficulties such a life must endure, Ally thought. Did she have a special bed or lie on her side waiting patiently for someone to turn her over? She looked as if she had been handsome in her time before the right-angle thing. He wondered what kept her going and left the goodness untouched. It must've been an effort to get ready for the evening.

A bell rang and they shuffled in to take their seats; however, there didn't seem to be any of the Chinese girls sitting near them. The orchestra absently strolled onto the stage with all the nonchalance of a philosophy symposium breaking for lunch. The audience settled down, yet the piano stool remained empty. Then without any discernible instruction, the orchestra started up in a haphazard way. It sounded as if they hadn't practised much. He checked his brochure – it was a symphony by Bartok and was meant to represent traffic. Ally reckoned he could've stayed at home for that. It wasn't relaxing and at one point, terror of his accident suddenly washed over him again. He was thankful when it eventually finished. There was a smattering of applause. Pages were turned.

Next, a man with a liver-coloured face and dressed as if he had something to do with horses sauntered on for his harpsichord solo. He explained that the composer had written it for the death of someone close to him, maybe a child, and that at the end, there was beautiful section as the soul ascended into heaven. With solemnity he began, yet it seemed as effortful as the heavy-handed washing of laundry in a river. To Ally's ears at least, the result was little different than could've been achieved from turning the handle of a machine that had a monkey on it.

When the interval eventually arrived, a sense of relief seemed to sweep through the audience. Usherettes appeared with trays of ice creams. Pockets were rummaged for change and handbags brought up onto knees. A loud cough then drew everyone's attention to the stage, and it was announced that Lang Lang had cancelled due to illness. The mood became subdued, and Ally felt for tortoise lady who he imagined was already struggling with the flip-down seating. He thought how music probably lifted her, taking her out of herself with a bodiless euphoria that was a taste of the heaven that was surely to come.

Jon mumbled something about going for a piss and Ally moved his knees to the side like a coy Victorian lady. As Jon made his way along the row, people popped up and down.

The Chinese students gathered in groups, checking their phones and a fat man made his way up the aisle as if moving an invisible wardrobe. Ally checked his watch, he felt Jon had been gone ages but in reality, it was only a few minutes. Out of nowhere, a feeling of loss overcame Ally and he thought how terrible it would be to grow up an orphan with so little tethering to this world.

Just as quickly, his attention was taken with a blind man being led to his seat by an attractive woman. There seemed to be a suffocating intimacy between them that couples have who share a tragedy. The man held onto her coat and Ally wondered if he could tell that the lights were on? Maybe by the heat or the bustle, people were like finches that started up when the blanket was removed. Maybe blind man regurgitated mashed up food for his wife – a blue-black tongue armless and sightless working it over like an escapologist trapped in a sack. Disappointingly, when they reached their seats, they didn't do anything unusual, just stared straight ahead even though there was nothing to see.

Jon was taking his time and he glanced over to the door with the green illuminated figure over it. Since his accident, Ally had little urge to eat or defecate and found it odd that others had to. At times his body felt little more than a meaty suit he had to wear. It was probably how divers felt getting into their wetsuits, a thick pealing on and off.

The Chinese boys were affecting a sort of 70's cool with slumped shoulders and tapping their programs against their legs like copies of the Racing Post. Blind guy had begun to pick at a scab on his neck, didn't he know that other people could see him? Even without the scab picking thing, he was no oil painting and Ally couldn't help thinking how cruel this irony was, with neither of them getting the benefit.

What could Jon be doing in there? The girls were sending texts with speed, and it was impressive the casual way they wore this skill. Blind guy was really picking away at his neck when he at last got hold of a loose bit of skin he was after. He sniffed it but not in an inquisitive way but as horses do, with hoovering nostrils that flared and quivered. Ally looked around him in astonishment to see if anyone else had noticed. But no one else was paying attention, not even with their extra strong glasses. Ally wondered whether blind man hoovered his wife like that in bed at night, inch by inch.

The lights went down, and Jon returned causing the row to pop up and down again. There was a damp patch clearly visible around his groin like the outline of Africa. The replacement pianist was as awkward as a teenager at her first prom. Yet, she sat with a ramrod posture and after a moment's composure, threw herself into the piece. Her fingers were a blur. Strong hands. She was putting effort into it, tensing through her arms and back when she pressed down on the keys like a masseur working on a particularly knotty back. Ally reckoned it must've been physically exhausting and he was impressed by her endurance as it seemed to go on forever. When the end came, she raised her arms as if breaking from a séance. Applause erupted and everyone stood.

"Enchanting but not spellbinding," Jon said.

Afterwards, they walked slowly home under a crocodile skin sky. People were still out and didn't even look sleepy. Ally's parents had always been in bed by 10, unless it was Christmas. Two shirtless men crisscrossed and sped past on roller skates, crouching forward and weaving between the crowd. Ally had never experienced the simple exhilaration and joy they showed, and he thought that only gay men lived for the moment like that. Stopping off for salt beef bagels at Sholom's, a light summer rain drifted in. And he thought of how tortoise lady would've probably liked to roller skate or even lift her cheeks to the rain.

"I saw an old man being dragged along by this middle-aged woman once," Jon said as if sensing Ally's thoughts. Ally had noticed that they had developed some sort of telepathy, a wordless talking between them. It was an intimacy that made Ally feel safe.

"She was probably his daughter."

"What made you think that?" Ally said.

"She looked like she didn't want to be there. As if she wasn't being paid and could do without it," Jon said opening his package and inspecting its contents closely. "There was nothing left of the guy." Jon took huge mouthful and between chews said, "He was like a glider made of brown paper and balsa that a gust of wind could've lifted into the air."

Ally pictured the paper-thin skin with veins showing through.

"He was an obstruction that wouldn't be there much longer."

Jon attacked his bagel, taking the next bite when his mouth was still half full.

"Life should be breath taking not just taking breaths," he said, fingering back in a slice of beef that hung from his lips like a second tongue.

Ally repeated this phrase in tune with their steps all the way home.

"The enemy's been in," Jon said as he pushed open the door.

Ally looked around but nothing had changed; the squalor was sprawled in the room much as before, like a fat man in a diaper.

Chapter 14

The radio played *Everybody Hurts* and Sarge leant
forward to turn it up. Diesel fumes rose as mist over
the Serengeti and schoolgirls hurtled after their bus.
Head buried deep in the bonnet of a car, the
mechanic at DG Autos looked like a tired dog with
a slipper in its mouth. A woman in a knitted hat
who'd come from a people bred in an airless place,
crossed the road carrying pale fruit. At the carwash,
they swarmed over a Mercedes and her face lost
deep in a puffy hoody, a young girl worked on the
front of the shiny black car. For a moment, she
stopped and stretched her back. Everybody hurts.

A seagull was laboriously crossing the sky
with little shoves, it made incremental headway.
Her gaze fell back to the earth-bound diesel smoke,
the man with the orange beard lounging at the door
of the second-hand fridge shop, the short woman in
the road and the policeman with the pitted face

staring out from his patrol car. All these people gathered together in this one place and time, God moving His chess pieces over the globe as the smoke rises.

And for a brief second, the girl breathed this world into her lungs and fleetingly, the infinite possibilities that would never be open to her were revealed. Then she seemed to fold it all away like a map into a knapsack before turning back to the rich man's shiny car.

Oh yes, everyone hurts and then hurts others, Sarge thought as he lifted the walkie talkie to his ear. It was hard for him to make out the crackling transmission and had to ask the controller to repeat the message. Then he slammed the Ford Fiesta into gear and screeched off. Rebecca rolled back like a fighter pilot pulling hard on the joystick and fries showered over her chest.

***

The hammering on the door was relentless and the shouts harsh and unfriendly. Ally turned up the volume on the TV, the neighbours had never been this angry before. When the door came through, it was like the breaching of a castle keep. Suddenly, too many overweight men were trying to get through the door in a hail of splinters that radiated from them as in religious iconography. It reminded Ally of a Guinness Book of Records attempt involving a telephone box or a mini. After a freezeframe moment, the dam burst and all hell broke loose. Ally's face was slammed into the carpet and a knee crushed his windpipe. His face was puckered up like a corrupted and haggard Botticelli cherub with rosebud lips. Jon rolled by in the tight embrace of someone wearing a fluorescent tabard. There must've been shouts but with his head pressed to the floor, all Ally heard were groans of a muffled and sinister intensity.

Sarge caught sight of Rebecca straddling Alistair Duncan as he rolled by. The irony of the situation wasn't lost on him as the sofa, ceiling, Rebecca and carpet furiously merged into one. From this spinning kaleidoscope of images, his mind picked out Rebecca's trousers which had ridden up to reveal her ankles. They didn't seem to taper but were stuffed into her orthopaedic shoes like badly fitting Ikea parts. He hit the wall and his spinning world came to a stop. Through sheer good fortune, Sarge found himself on top, and he swiftly cuffed the arm that was stuck in his face. But when he searched for the other one, he couldn't find it anywhere. Rebecca was now chatting away to the desk sergeant who'd come along for the ride, and who'd munched away happily on his sandwiches before the van had even left.

Jon was cursing and trying to bite Sarge as he patted around looking for the elusive arm. In the end, he cuffed Jon's left wrist to his right ankle, jumping clear like a game show contestant who'd successfully completed a time-dependent task. But no one was watching, and the struggle had exhausted his scarred lungs as he tried to get his breath back. The forensic team were soon about their work and fussing around him.

It was with some reluctance that he considered the mundane business of finishing the arrest. The suspect would need to be loaded into the van and gotten back to the station, where endless paperwork lay in front of him. Sarge wasn't looking forward to tackling Jon again who was frothing at the mouth like some inbred backwoodsman who'd lost his banjo.

With a sigh, Sarge began searching his belt first with one hand then with both, it was with mounting panic that they urgently shuffled back and forth. The keys to the cuffs weren't anywhere to be found. They must've come off in the struggle. Fortunately, no one was paying him any attention yet, and quickly he was down on his knees peering under the sofa. Among the lunar landscape, he found a hard and yellow peanut and tuppence coin but no keys. He started pulling off the sofa cushions but was shouted at by a woman in a face mask and blue body suit. Now everyone was looking.

In the end, four of them had to carry the trussed-up hippy to the van. Jon was twisting and knotting, and kicked one of the guys in the nuts. Then in turn, Sarge was punched by the man with the sore privates who made his way out as if in some PTA sack-race. The apoplectic desk sergeant made Sarge ride in the back with the prisoner.

It was a long drive and Sarge tried to put himself far away, where he was with Arshad, the window was open and the summer breeze was scented from the jasmine bush and passing girls swayed like a dashboard, hula-dancing doll. The conversation eventually turned away from his incompetence to the match on Sky that evening, and he closed his eyes. It was then that he heard a faint, ethereal tinkle like finger symbols. Looking up he saw Rebecca smirking at him through the grill. She was holding up a couple of silver keys that glistened and danced in the sun.

***

Across town, Greg stared at Fran as she drifted in and out of sleep. Her hair seemed to be held in shape by static like a ball of candy floss. It seemed to be barely attached to the off-white eggshell of her head. How thin her skull seemed and with a pale membrane covering. He imagined how easy it would be to smash open, causing brightly coloured smarties to spill over the floor as if from an easter egg. In fact, it didn't seem that farfetched to Greg, reckoning with all the pills she'd taken in her time.

She stirred and her dentures had moved to reveal blackened stubs, all the sins and corruption of their plans seemed made flesh in that ruinous mouth. Then, before he knew what he was doing, his hands were round her throat. Greg lifted her off her feet and her face grew red and bloated, he pressed harder and shook her back and forth. His

154

fingers ached but he didn't let up until he heard a cracking sound like a cat with a chicken carcass. It seemed to take no time at all for her to go limp and he let her drop to the floor, her lifeless body forming a question mark to something she hadn't had time to ask. What could he answer anyway? Nothing. There was no reason or explanation he could give.

Slumped in the armchair, he swung the vodka bottle. After years of patience and careful planning, he had finally snapped. True, it had been one of his options, but not like this, not in his flat, and not with a corpse to dispose of. As he drank, he calmed. Then slowly, he became aware of a sound that made him think of a prisoner sawing away at the bars. Short, furious strokes. He looked around but nothing moved. Then Greg realized it was his own breathing, and he was reminded again how out of condition he had become. Broken veins spread across his nose and nowadays his father stared back at him from the mirror. It was as if Fran had infected him with her virus.

All of a sudden, Greg had an inexplicable urge to defecate. He eased himself up and on the way to the toilet, he kicked the lifeless body with his remaining strength. Air wheezed out of her like a deflating leather football. His actions were shocking to him – not with the murder, which was clearly justified, but by kicking the body. How quickly he'd become able to act without feelings, at least for others. The shame and indignity of his own existence were crystal clear to him as he unbuckled with clumsy actions and his trousers dropped to the floor.

Still wheezing, he settled down and tried to rationalise what had just happened. But no thoughts came to him, there was only a hyper-awareness of things, such as his thin and pale legs that stuck out from beneath his belly. The drip from within the cistern echoed like the limestone drops in a cave, white as saliva. Greg had heard of burglars leaving a turd floating in the properties they robbed. This he could understand; the nerves, excitement, relief and revenge – but what he couldn't understand was why they didn't wipe? Maybe they needed more fibre in their diet? After he'd finished, he made sure he cleaned himself thoroughly to distinguish himself from a common criminal and flushed the handle repeatedly like a Lowestoft fishwife beheading herring. Afterall, it was he who would have to return to it later.

Re-entering the lounge, he was struck by the feeling that something wasn't right. At first, he couldn't work out what it might be; the sunken armchair squatted much as before as if it too was having a dump, the table covered in prints and cold mugs of grey tea with his brushes like bamboo in a toxic lake, the milk stool on its side and canvasses stacked against the wall. Everything in its place as he mentally ticked them off… except no murder victim.

He played it again through his head; sleep, wake, throttle, body onto the floor with its tongue hanging out as if waiting for one last pill, and finally the shit. Nope, there was definitely meant to be a body in the scene. Then it occurred to him – had death come just a bit too quick? After all, junkies were crafty and dogged, and as he knew from all her near-death stories, they just never gave up. Like zombies, you could lop off limbs and they would still come for their fix, dragging their mutilations behind them. Could she have played dead? How was he to know; he hadn't killed anyone before.

When he noticed the open front door, an unexpected energy surged through him and before he knew it, he was heading down the stairs. His feet were dancing as if controlled by a deranged puppeteer. Greg almost fell into the street and was immediately struck but how eerily empty it was. A fox trotted down the middle of the road on tiptoe and the only sound was the low hum of a far-off generator that was most likely keeping something in this world. If only just with its solitary labour.

For no particular reason, he chose to go left and began to run. It was no better than last time, being awkward and heavy. He concluded running was something to be put aside with childhood. When he reached the first corner, there was still no sign. He put his head down and started off again. Slaps rang out mournfully into the night air as if a club hostess was working on a customer she had little enthusiasm for. At the next junction, he caught sight of Fran. It hadn't been much of a chase at all; nonetheless, he had to hold onto the wall as he got his breath back. Her neck was at a strange angle, and she kept hitting the wall like a broken wind-up toy. She had made even less headway than him.

Greg caught up with her in a few strides and his measured walking seemed faster than his attempts at running had. When she saw him loom out of the night, she slid to the floor and curled into a ball.

"There you are."

She was staring up at him.

"You had some sort of seizure and banged your head. I went to fetch some paracetamol and when I got back, you'd disappeared."

She mouthed something he didn't catch.

"Have you hurt your neck? It looks funny."

There was a moment's self-doubt in her eyes. It was impossible to guess how many bad trips or psychotic episodes she'd had, delusions that doctors and therapists later showed her to be untrue. She must doubt herself on every level, he thought.

"Here, let me help," Greg said scooping her up in his arms. "You can't be too careful with head injuries, they can turn nasty. Look what happened to brain... I mean Alistair."

She was no weight at all. She seemed dead already.

"The ambulance is on its way. It's probably there now waiting for us."

When they turned the corner, there were no blue flashing lights or stretcher being unfolded like an ironing-board. Her impassive eyes never left him as they climbed the stairs. They were both resigned to their fates. A feint smell of faeces lingered in the air as they entered the flat, and the open door made it seem as if the place was airing itself. He placed her on the sofa where she shivered.

"I'll make tea," he said. "Tea is the universal panacea for all ills. Then I'll run a bath and when you're soaking, I'll change the sheets so it will be nice and fresh for you."

Neither of them mentioned the ambulance.

Only then did she close her eyes.

Greg went to the kitchen and put the kettle on. He took two mugs out of the cupboard before putting one back. Then he searched through the draws, picking out the biggest knife he could find. He went back into the lounge and without a word launched himself at her in a frenzy. The knife made a squelching sound like water in a Wellington boot.

161

Blood covered his hands and face and sprayed up the walls. He didn't stop until all that was left was the red fleshy lump of unidentifiable roadkill that had been run over many times. Then he sat in his armchair and had that nice cup of tea.

***

The cell was better than hospital. Ally had a toilet to himself and more attention. They took his belt and he had to hold up his trousers like a poacher carrying rabbits. There is, however, a general indignity and a lack of privacy when dealing with any institutions. They are services a person paid for but never wanted to collect on. Throughout the night, doors slammed, and drunks had shouted and wept for all they'd lost. In the morning, he ate sausage and baked beans with a plastic knife/fork/spoon-in-one instrument. It was like being in a Wendy house as a grown-up – awkward and not wholly right.

On the way to questioning, he'd passed the Asian policeman who'd stared at him with the hatred of a wronged man. Ally had smiled in return; after all, it was what the Dali Lama would've wanted him to do. There was no need for a solicitor, Ally could barely remember his name let alone where he was on certain dates. He wondered why Jon had been brought in too, probably for resisting arrest. But then again, Jon resisted life in general and especially happiness, he resisted that with all his heart.

There had been raised voices, papers slammed on the tabletop and a cassette recorder with a red light that glowed like an addict's e-cigarette. As a teenager, Ally taped the top twenty countdown from the radio on Sunday evenings. He'd had to press the record and play buttons simultaneously on a Phillips RR712 which had the recoil of an AK47. He remembered that no matter how hard he tried, he'd always caught a fragment of the inane DJ trying to bring some gravity to his juvenile job.

Through hours of interview, Ally grinned impassively and each time an exasperated inquisitor had reached their limit, they were replaced by someone more senior. Eventually, a tired-looking man with a porous nose and face like a motorway map turned up. Ally thought he was the sort of person who had his own pewter tankard behind the bar at a pub which had books that no one read. The man sighed heavily and there were wet patches under the arms of a nylon shirt. Ally pictured him, after a hard day, soaking the nose in whisky like others would their chilblains. Let the nose drink first. The same questions were gone over yet again. After another night in the cells, he was reluctantly released.

Jon was waiting for him at reception. It was as if they were finishing detention together.

As they crossed forecourt, Ally said, "How'd it go?"

"I tied them up in knots."

"Me too."

The flagstones were tilted like a frozen sea and Sarge stared down from the fourth floor with dismay and anger. They had the cocky saunter of young men fresh from the barbers. The Metropolitan Police flag struggled in the wind like a man trying to change a duvet cover.

Sarge was as lonely as he'd been at school; in fact, the station with its weather-bleached cladding and concrete cancer could've easily been mistaken for any failing comprehensive. A passer-by looking up at that moment would've seen a youngish man with his forehead pressed against a window, and one who'd felt powerless his whole life against the petty bigotry that persevered in both institutions. His fists came up and silently pounded away at glass pane.

***

'Be nice', Greg had said, she would show him nice alright. And when Ally turned up this time with his story of being arrested and spending the night in jail, she had almost been impressed. Still, she had to get very drunk before she let him get near her. Even then, he was so broken it was she who had had to grab him by the shirt and push his hands into her pants, where he fumbled around as if trying to pick fluff off a woolly sweater.

Growing up, she'd had a bullterrier called Boston who would lay on his back showing the pink and black place where his knackers used to be. The whole sad, loveless act had brought Boston back to mind and filled her with the only trace of real sentiment she'd felt in years. Afterwards, he was panting and with idiotic grin on his face.

"You better not have come inside me," Maggie said.

***

Sarge's mum had liked Iqbal, the name she would've chosen. She said how she'd been promised a successful man with prospects, not one who worked in a factory. When she met him, she wanted to get the first flight back to Pakistan and sit again with her father under their fig tree. The Khyber hills were snow-capped this time of year. Her mother-in-law had persuaded her to stay and marry, and what she ended up with was a disease that would kill her children. Disappointment was the weave that bound the family together, Sarge thought as he sipped his tea. Snatches of conversation from the pavement outside washed over him like the tuning of a wartime radio. She had made biryani for him to take back to his cadet quarters.

Chapter 15

The white clapboards and plastic flowers gave the crematorium something of small-town America, the only thing missing was the well-coiffured realtor flashing a Hollywood smile. Ally could see Fran slapping her thigh with a *yeeha*. She'd spent days on end sleeping in St Martins in the field, but she'd found it dark and oppressive. Said the saints and gargoyles had peered down on her through the gloom like spear fishermen, and the eagerness in their eyes had made her uneasy. That memory had followed her ever since like a loyal cow, she'd said.

All religious art was like the Sistine Chapel to Ally where everything was the colour of the sea and nobody had many clothes on, but for Fran it was more like a chilly day out in Southend and with the subjects suffering knife wounds. No, for her paradise was a shack not a mansion. Well, she might not have gotten her shack, Ally thought, but at least she has a Colonial-style condo.

Ally and Jon sat to the left wearing the same clothes they had for the concert, and Jon had asked whether there would be a buffet. There was only a smattering of people who didn't seem to know each other. Some quietly sobbed; their backs were going up and down as if they were being frisked by an invisible hand.

"They weep for themselves," Jon said.

When the music started, the sparse gathering turned to watch the coffin brought in. Weddings and funerals, everyone wanted a sight of the star of the show. The undertakers seemed to carry their burden with remarkable ease as if Fran's worries were much of her earthly weight and had now passed from her. However, they had trouble keeping in step and it all seemed a bit amateurish. As they reached the front, they put the coffin down like weightlifters after a good lift, dropping it the last bit and stepping back smartly. Ally thought he heard something scrape inside.

The burgundy curtains behind the priest made him seem like a compare for an amateur dramatic society in the provinces. Shuffling his papers and struggling with a persistent dry cough, he looked as if he'd forgotten the next act. Yet, after doublechecking he had the right notes, he launched with quiet determination into summing up a person he'd never met.

There was a story about ballet classes and apparently early promise, passing a scholarship to the Guildhall Music School before discovering Janis Joplin and a taste for self-destruction. Of the hated piano lessons and a recording of her practicing that she played loud in her bedroom while getting high, her parents only realising when the same mistake came up repeatedly. Her dad put an arm round her mum at this memory.

The priest took his time; after all, what was the hurry? Eventually the curtains opened, and the coffin began to trundle off like at a supermarket checkout. Fran's mum wailed and her dad stood and bowed. *Amazing Grace* came through the little speaker that set up on a pole. It had the temporary feel of a gymkhana, something set up by good-willed parents and would suffer reverberating feedback at crucial moments. Despite this, when he heard the words, *I once was lost but now am found,* hot tears flowed down Ally's cheeks.

A general drift set in and slowly, people began to collect up their bags as if surprised it was over. Some had taken the opportunity to do a bit of shopping while they were out. Ally and Jon were the last ones seated.

"The first time I met her parents," Ally said, "they had the air of people generally expecting the worst."

Jon fidgeted.

"Fran had a niece's christening, and she was coming down the stairs in different outfits. Putting on a show. She paraded back and forth as we sat at the breakfast table drinking coffee, then stamping her foot, she'd run off for the next outfit. Her parents' faces shone."

The priest had already changed into a raincoat, the zip was stuck, and he was jerking at it ineffectually. Ally couldn't help noticing he had trainers on.

"I was caught up in it too," he continued. "She was like a benevolent dictator. The knock-kneed run up the stairs holding her dress."

It was probably one of the few happy and innocent moments they'd shared. "There was also something easily hurt in her and even back then, I think I knew she would never be happy. The world would turn on her and bring her down like wounded prey. It sniffs out weakness like that and destroys it. Like eating the runt of the litter, the nutrients recycled."

It was the most he'd said in one go since his accident.

Jon lifted a buttock and farted.

In the carpark, a handful of people mingled as if reluctant to depart. Fran's parents shook the last damp hands as the ever-dwindling family shuffled off. A bearish man with a paint-flecked shirt who no one seemed to know looked them sincerely in the eyes and said, "An old friend."

Then he unexpectedly hugged her father and kissed the shocked mother on the lips.

Autumn leaves scurried along the pavement, first in little individual bursts and then with a collective surge. Only recently, Ally had seen a programme about tardigrades, creatures like microscopic armour-plated pigs that could even live on the moon curled up in balls as the hostile winds rush past them. He thought these would probably move like the autumn leaves. Fran's parents looked desolate, and their eyes seemed to implore Ally for some scintilla of comfort. But he doubted they would want to hear about tardigrades. Most likely, they would rather hear something about Fran. Without a word, he turned and walked out of their lives forever. And like the leaves, Ally didn't know what to do or where to go next.

Chapter 16

There had been no worthwhile forensics. No DNA matches with anyone apart from The Chuckle Brothers and one unknown male. There was nothing to suggest that Fran Duncan had ever been at the flat let alone met a grisly end there. Sarge repeatedly scanned the microfiche of little grey squares until they merged together into a very dull *What the Butler Saw,* there wasn't even a chunky toothless woman removing an ankle stocking.

"I'm just going to do him myself. Fuck collecting evidence. Once I did a favour for someone, who knows someone…" Sarge's blood surged through him carrying his disease like a tidal wave did bodies, a tumbling confusion of noughts and crosses. "I've got contacts in the nether regions."

"Underworld," Rebecca said her thumbs dancing over her phone, "nether regions is something else, dickhead."

***

The just-after-rain feeling reminded Ally of shopping with his mum on Saturday mornings with its forest of coats flapping against his face like miserable earthbound ghosts. The Arndale Centre was a haven of light and life for her, already numbed with an early morning a vodka and two Quiet Life. Her soft hand had slipped from his decades ago now.

***

The puckering oil hissed and turned ochre as Greg threw Sicilian sausage into the pan. Then he broke four eggs into a mug and beat them with a fork. Membrane trailed over the kitchen top like the goo from an orgy. With the flick of the wrist, he tossed the crisping sausage slices and turned down the heat as the oil spat over his bare stomach.

Cooking naked made him feel like the artist that painting never did. With a tea towel, he cleaned round his genitals like a mechanic polishing a replaced part. He poured the eggs into the saucepan and stirred it round with a wooden spoon. Maggie was in the shower, and he called out to her but without reply. After setting the plates and coffee on the table, he settled on a chair and his bare arse spread over the stool as smooth as pancake mix. He shouted to Maggie again. Funerals gave him such an appetite.

Water cascaded over Maggie, and she scrubbed away at herself furiously as if trying to remove radioactive contamination. But there was no cleaning some memories, they were branded on her soul. It was the third test she'd flushed down the toilet before storming out, a towel wrapped round her head like a meringue.

"That's it! No more pissing around, the little wanker must die."

"What's happened?" Greg said between mouthfuls.

Corpses seemed to be stacking up like kindling.

***

They stared into the middle distance and for once, neither of them had turned the TV on. "This particular time it was serious, and Fran was wired up like a synthetic in a sci-fi film. This machine was sucking away blood clots. It's a close thing but you sort of got used to it after a while, like racing drivers and crashes, I guess."

Ally manipulated the remote as a drummer counting in the rest of the band.

"Jeremiah from B10 suddenly wheels himself in at full speed demanding a pen and paper. 'I've got a chick's number, I need to get it down'.

He's so excited, he tears off a corner from the notes at the end of her bed and a stubby biro appears out of nowhere. Mouthing the number as he writes and then holds it up like a winning lottery ticket."

Ally smiled to himself as others would the fond recollection of a country drive or weekend in Hove.

"He counter rotates the wheels and does a couple of circles, the scrap of paper in his mouth. Fran doesn't even know he's there but Jeremiah's whooping away and cries out, 'The trap's been set and she's in for the shag of her life.' All the while his stump's sticking out and a drainage bag full of puss is swinging under his chair."

Ally looked over but Jon didn't show any sign of having heard a word.

"On the whole, they were high-spirited on the amputee ward," Ally said.

Chapter 17

Abandoned paintings were strewn over the floor and pots overturned, the chaos was even more unbalancing than the three-legged milking stool Sarge was perched on. Greg was doodling away in a notebook as if he hadn't a care in the world. Every so often he would work away at the charcoal with a blackened thumb. Sarge couldn't gather his thoughts. He knew that some cultures believed that photography stole a person's soul but what about a drawing? Would it take it bit by bit like picking at spaghetti with chopsticks? Suppose it didn't look like him, would the soul of someone who happened to look more like the picture be lost? Perhaps if he took it home, the disease would eat away at the picture rather than him, but Sarge knew Dorian Grey wasn't for poor Asian kids from the Beaumont Estate. One thing he was sure of though, that bloody scratching was stealing what little concentration and essential being he still had left.

"Why are you asking me about events and individuals I know nothing of?" Greg said.

"It's routine," although Sarge couldn't remember asking him anything much at all.

"How did you get my name?"

"Your girlfriend is screwing Mr Duncan," Sarge said without intending to. He was shocked by his own bluntness.

"Maggie and the lame fuck landlord? I don't think so."

Scratch, scribble, scratch.

"The evidence would suggest."

"What evidence?"

"I'm not at liberty."

"Then how should I know?"

"Know what?"

"Anything."

Scratch, scratch scribble.

The conversation went round in a dizzying circle, Duncan, Jon, Maggie and did he know Fran?

"Who?"

"Fran Duncan."

"Dr Who's assistant?"

"Eh?"

"Hey."

"Hey?"

"Nonny Nonny," Greg said and when he judged it would be most annoying, he worked at the paper furiously as if doing a brass rubbing. It wouldn't take much to almost feel sorry for the Asian policeman with the pock-marked face, he seemed tired and lost. But Greg was having way too much fun to stop.

Sarge could hear Rebecca lifting and dropping heavy objects in the other rooms. There were thuds and oaths and the breathy intimacy usually found in boxing clubs. Sarge could feel her strength through the walls, the endless outdoor sports of a privileged education would stand a person in good stead in that regard. Sarge closed his notepad, yet he hadn't written anything down. At the same time, Greg stopped doodling, blew on the book and laid it face down. It was as if two duellers had backed down from the final standoff and decided to go home.

Rebecca came through shaking her head. There was a sudden stillness as if no one seemed to know what to do next. Greg wondered what would happen if he suddenly jumped up from his chair and grabbed the sturdy policewoman to start a makeshift conga line? He had always wondered at the innocent spontaneity that Down's people possess.

Rebecca produced a sample bag from her pocket.

"We need a swab."

"What for?" Greg suddenly alert.

"For elimination purposes."

"Eliminating from what?"

"Our enquiries."

"Enquiries into what?"

"There's been a murder."

"Of whom?"

"Fran Duncan."

"Who?"

It occurred to Greg that maybe someone had recognised him at the crematorium, but he quickly discounted this. There had hardly been anyone there, and those that were more interested in navigating their shopping trolleys down the steps without losing any of the morning's charity shop bargains. Besides, he'd been disguised in a Columbo pervert's mac and had fitted right in.

"Will you give us a sample?"

"It will be a cold day in hell before that cotton bud gets anywhere near one of my orifices."

Rebecca shrugged and went to the sink to wash her hands.

Was that it? Sarge stared at her. Surely, there was more that could be done. Threaten him with a warrant or court order, put a cup or glass in an evidence bag, or swab something? Anything.

Even if they binned everything when they got outside. Give him something to think about. Sarge'd seen such things on *Law and Order* but Rebecca just didn't seem much bothered about anything as she dried her fingers methodically with the filthy tea towel.

***

Since the cremation, Ally had taken to watching *Songs of Praise* and irregularly going to Mass. Fran's had been the first funeral he'd been to since his parents' car crash, which had been more like a birthday party, just with more tears. Hugs from aunties and uncles ruffling his hair. There had been ham sandwiches and Ribena. When Ally had first sheepishly poked his head into the church, it'd been like visiting another country with its own language and unfamiliar customs, but without the sunstroke or stomach upset. Jon sometimes went with Ally, where he would wear a crash helmet as if expecting the worst. Maybe he thought he might meet an Asian girl there. After all, they had taken to Catholicism as they had to the bicycle – with a sober resolution.

St Michael's of Moorfields was underground, the walls were a prison grey gloss that looked easy to wipe down and a crayon rainbow was above the door. The congregation was mostly from the Peabody estate and the priest attended pastoral duties at Pentonville. A decrepit old lady would wheeze away at the organ like Ivor Cutler and an Italian man in a bad toupee led the singing and seemed the only one who could read the words.

Morning service and sunlight would be scrunched around the altar like the yellow cellophane in shoe shops of provincial towns. Things took time to get going, rolling forward as painfully as a truck pull in World's Strongest Man. Ally would stand, kneel and sit with everyone else, engaging in the slow calisthenics session for the soul.

He discovered it provided the same security his parents' bungalow had many years ago. Once a year, they would have akelas from scouts over for a cheese and wine party, where they'd had pickled onions on sticks. His mother would dress up and have trouble manoeuvring the hostess trolley through the doors. It'd been unsettling seeing akelas out of uniform and they were diminished by it. Ally would lay in the dark listening to the laughter coming around the walls.

Bending and stretching, the words and effort thickened the air like flour to water. And when the *peace be with you* arrived, there was always a collective sigh of relief, as if putting a common burden down. People smiled, shook his hand and genuinely seemed to wish them well. Jon would bump fists with unsuspecting pensioners and said, 'safe'. Then it would be back to it, faces serious again, intent on their own internal struggles.

Ally's favourite place to sit was next to the jugs of water and wine on a small table at the back.

They had cling film over them which Ally reckoned probably prevented the Holy Spirit evaporating. One time the jugs had been carried forward by a lady in an electric wheelchair who sped forward apparently with little accelerator control. Her head had wobbled like a nodding dog.

When the queue for communion patiently shuffled forward, it was over for them. He and Jon never went up. Sometimes Ally would pop Rennie from its silver pack and quietly pray for Fran's peaceful repose as it dissolved into a grainy, minty mush on his tongue. It was amongst these refugees from life that Ally and Jon had finally found a home.

***

Sunday afternoons Ally couldn't wait to be over, it was like the awkward waiting for someone to pass. They were watching the cars in the Abu

188

Dhabi Grand Prix whizz round pointlessly. The crashes seemed as insignificant as if they were toys.

"When scientists predict the future, it's only the shit things that come true," Jon was saying. "Floods, over population, food shortages, wars, pestilence, forest fires, millions on the move, all came to pass."

Genius often chose unlikely places to dwell, Ally thought, and probably to shop as well. The British Heart Foundation outlets were the best, but their products were often bulky.

"But where are the flying cars, the cures for cancer and the hot android serving wenches?"

Jon was staring at Ally like a fake psychic trying to move a glass across the table. Under the scrutiny, Ally became even more nonplussed and no thought came to him. Which wasn't unusual.

"In Abu fucking Dhabi, that's where!" Jon shouted.

"I knew that."

Jon leaned forward and pointed to the screen as the camera angle cut to the stands, "Look at the beautiful people high up in their glass pod. They're a different species from the rest of us."

Ally stared transfixed at the glowing women.

"The news is full of the displaced sliding out of deflating dinghies, their whole world a carrier bag and mobile phone."

The same as us, Ally thought.

Images of untouchable women gazing down like emperors as the desperate fought each other to survive whirled through his mind. The golden ones sipping cocktails and laughing.

"There's no endless youth or robot helpers with perky breasts," Jon said. The apocalypse is here and the barricades are going up, the rich are in their towers and the poor tearing each other apart for a mouthful of food or medicine. Abu Dhabi, holiday playground of footballers and home of the night-time Grand Prix, is the end of the world."

Chapter 18

The following weekend and Maggie posed on the bonnet of the borrowed Clio, sticking out her tits and ass like on the KP nuts poster in a backstreet garage. She put one hand behind her head and lifted a knee, turned round and looked over her shoulder. Ally said she was Bonnie to his Clyde as he clicked away taking photos with her phone. She gritted her teeth. Everything about him made her skin crawl. In her mind, she was a real trouper, stoically smiling and finishing the routine as boos and catcalls rained down on her. Fuck, he was holding onto that bloody carrier bag like it was a Prada handbag.

When she'd had just about all she could take, she tugged down her skirt in the same practical manner she would remove bubble-wrap from a new TV and headed off.

***

"Are you sure about this?" Jon had said.

Out of the blue, Maggie had called the bat phone and said she wanted to go to the coast, that she had always liked cliffs. It was her favourite thing to stand near the edge and watch the sea lunge and growl beneath. Her words, lunge and growl, like a lion cub practising its hunting, Ally thought.

"A date?"

"It's not a fucking date," she'd said.

Ally's dad had once taken him to Old Harry Rocks and they'd both lain down to look over the edge. Ally's heart had pounded in his chest like a mad aunt locked in the attic and his head had swum. He'd worn a red jumper with a white, zig-zag pattern across the chest. For some reason, it bothered him now that he couldn't remember what happened to that jumper. He'd never understood that things were ever fully lost, a small bit of him always held out hope.

"You know she was the bitch who grassed you up to the filth," Jon said.

"I know," Ally said as he smoothed his hair in the mirror.

Jon went to the kitchen and handed over a bag without a word. Ally peered inside: there were two tin foil parcels and a bottle of cherry aid. Jon rolled a cigarette one-handed. Like juggling, it was a skill Ally was amazed anyone could master. Picking a loose strand of tobacco from his lips, Jon turned back to Master Chef.

"Well, it's your life, even if it is a sad excuse for one," Jon said.

After some thought, Ally pulled a rumpled envelope from his pocket, handed it to Jon and left.

On the envelope was:

To be opened ONLY!!! in the event of my demise.

There were four red asterisks framing the writing, drawn with a red marker-pen. They were like squashed mosquitoes and had stained through to the back of the envelope. *Demise*, who used a word like that apart from a character in a Jane Austin novel, Jon thought? He was manipulating the envelope like a chimp with a makeup mirror.

***

She could hear him hurrying after her like an eager pet with too-short legs, maintaining enough distance between them so she didn't have to look at him. In the 40 minutes they'd been heading along the top of the cliffs, they hadn't passed even a single dog-walker or earnest rambler. Eventually, she chose a spot that was the same as many others that they'd passed. It was slight hollow that couldn't be seen from the path should someone happen along. Seagulls wheeled overhead staring down at them with child-pharaoh eyes.

They sat watching the sea. It rose and fell, and Ally thought it was sleeping. At one point, geese crested the hilltop behind them in bomber formation and headed out to sea. They made a sound like creaking timbers and many men rowing. But that was pretty much all that happened, and time hung heavy. Even by his standards, it was dull.

Maggie shook off her shoes. Dirt from the walk had stained her toes as if they were partially drawn in charcoal. It was as if Greg had brought her to life, smudging and shading with his thumb before losing interest. Maggie felt he had put her aside with the intention of reworking some details later but had never got back to it. She angled her feet to get a better, more rounded impression. They could definitely have done with more attention, a bit smaller and maybe less masculine.

Rummaging in the carrier bag, Ally pulled out two foil packages. In Jon's future world, he wasn't one of the beautiful people and would be jostling over scraps. But Ally also knew he lacked the strength or will to fight, and there would be no place for him in a world like this.

Holding out the packages, Ally said, "Ham and mustard or cheese and piccalilli?"

Maggie looked at him as if he was offering her a choice between the faeces of two different animals. Waving him away, she produced a can of Guinness from her coat pocket. As she opened it, white foam erupted from the can and in a swift movement, she managed to cover the top of the can with the whole of her mouth. It was like a snake swallowing a sheep.

Ally opened the ham and began to eat slowly. Maggie had spread her legs to set herself, she was strong and capable.

A lone seagull lethargically took off from the cliffs and headed towards a far-off fishing boat in an unhurried manner. The crew were hauling crab-pots and looked as if they were pulling at a giant plug. Ally imagined a vortex of water sucking down the trawler, seagull, sky, cliffs and lastly them, with one big burp. But nothing stirred, apart from the slow undulation of sea and sky.

Maggie tossed the can aside and sighed deeply. It was now or never. She double-checked where he'd put the car keys – in the breast pocket of his out-of-date safari jacket, which was now being held down by the cherry aid like a squashed animated character. The second can she opened foamed less and she drank nearly half of it in one go. Ally was mesmerised by her throat moving in and out like a fakir climbing a rope.

"What?" she said, wiping her mouth.

Maggie got to her feet, brushing grass from her clothes. How she hated those puppy eyes that stared up at her, besotted and brainless. She took a couple of steps to the cliff edge and peered over. In her mind, she saw herself performing the self-same act Greg had a few months previously at the taxi rank. But this time succeeding, unlike that useless bastard. Ally came up to her shoulder as she knew he would.

A Sea Cat ferry loomed over the horizon and crossed slowly in front of them. It looked like it had been designed by a child with a set square. She was aware of the smallest things. A bumble bee clambering up a flower stem that failed to hold its weight and it fell backwards. The salt-crusted weeds were like Christmas cake decorations and an unknown creature's poo as hard as buckshot.

Maggie suddenly grabbed his coat. The Guinness can dropped and a pale sausage of tripe-coloured fluid coiled out as it bounced over into the abyss as loathsome as the unexpected and revolting disembowelling of a small creature. She heaved with all her strength and before Ally knew what was happening, he was star-fishing out into nothingness. Flailing desperately, he caught only air as a look of disbelief and betrayal contorted his face. He was attempting a half-hearted front crawl, churning the air as a mechanical bath toy would the soap suds. Tumbling away, his hurt and crying eyes met hers as the waves caught him *thud* like a giant, blue baseball glove.

Silence.

The bee was on its back moving its legs as if performing a sedentary form of Thai Chi for the infirm.

But when she turned round, Ally was still standing there much as before, docile and compliant. In reality, she hadn't moved. She was worse than Greg, at least he'd tried. And to cap it all, the idiot was staring back at her with the big eyes and tangled hair of a child who didn't understand his place in this world.

It would be an adoption more than a partnership. Strange to think that this boy was father to her unborn child. She would be nursing the two of them for rest of her life, one hanging from each breast. They would be like ticks that gorge themselves, yet these would never fall off. It was probably her damned hormones that had stopped her throwing this dead weight over the edge, and this is what she told herself as she stormed off cursing his name.

Without looking back, Maggie knew that he would be scrabbling around, collecting what was left of their pathetic picnic and hurrying after her. She felt like a gambler who was in the middle of the biggest losing streak of their life. A plane emerged from the hazy sky like something half remembered and then with a roar of its engines, faded away again taking with it the hope and collective anticipation of adventure of those onboard.

***

They hadn't exchanged a word all the way back, yet Ally was utterly content and at peace, which only made her even more angry. People too easily pleased were always despised. She could barely stand his very presence as she picked away at the flaking polish on her nails. Where there was no varnish, she picked at nail. The 'fuck, fuck, fuck, fuck, fuck, fuck' going through her head was like an iron stake being driven in. Each blow made her wince.

Abruptly, she stood up and held onto the worktop. Could she do this? After all, everyone else did, settling for incomplete lives with people they couldn't stand. It went on generation after generation. Besides, it wasn't as if her life had been so great up until this point.

Straightening, Maggie began banging cupboards and set about making something to eat. Water sprayed over her as she filled the pans. Had the water always been that powerful in the taps, or had they decided to conspire against her like everything else today? She slammed the saucepans on the stove and worked away at the can-opener like she was wringing a cockerel's neck. Carrots were chopped with ferocity and rounds flew off into the sink. After 20mins or so, a break unexpectedly appeared in the cooking preparations, and it surprised her see the various pots were boiling away quite merrily. Maybe it would be like this, snatched moments of relief when she needed it most. Just enough to keep her going as the days stretched before her as endless as a desert road. Numbness had descended on her that was not unlike contentment. She could do this. She juggled another Guinness as if deciding what to do next.

Then, amid all this unexpected optimism, it fell from her hands, bounced and split, and out came the same pale sausage of intestines she'd seen earlier on the cliffs. Like all Catholics, Maggie was superstitious and she couldn't help but think it was some sort of premonition. Of what she couldn't fathom but still crossed herself furiously.

It occurred to Ally that he should call Jon to let him know he was OK and staying with Maggie. But he hadn't replaced his mobile after the accident and didn't want to ask to borrow Maggie's and risk spoiling the mood. Not now that everything was going so well. She was even cooking dinner, although he wasn't sure about the combination of ingredients he'd seen on the work top. But who knew; maybe cloves, cream and tinned spaghetti would come together?

***

"They were coming out of Nisa's, this family, and there must've been maybe 8 kids, I guess, though it was hard to be sure. The tallest at the front and smallest at the back," Sarge said as Rebecca flicked between the radio stations. He was long past caring what she thought of him. If anything. The more she ignored him, the more he wanted to irritate her.

"The fat mum was out front and then the kids who all had the same face. Smooth and round like an egg but with meat-tearing teeth. It was *Deliverance* come to Croydon."

Popping open the lid of his Tupperware box, biryani smells filled the Ford Focus. He saw Rebecca pull a face. Sarge reckoned Indian food was OK after a skin-full of lager on a Friday night but not in the car or next door.

"The one at the back was struggling with his bag and was using both hands. He looked as if he wanted to escape but a force held him there," Sarge re-sealed the lid, pressing round the edges and then the last corner. "Some sort of lethargy or in-bred sluggishness seemed to be clogging their veins."

Rebecca's mobile phone pinged like a microwave, and she set to at it with her thumbs.

"What did you get?" she mumbled.

"Eh?"

"From Nisa."

"Nothing, I was just window shopping."

Sarge tossed the lunchbox in the back, and it bounced around with surprising force. He'd forgotten it was still full.

"I guess there is no escaping where you come from," he said.

"They had messed up blood like yours."

A moment after the lights in the flat went out, a hunched figure could be seen scampering along the gutter. Sarge pulled on his gloves and glanced at Rebecca who was still texting away. She was holding the phone with the forceful grip of someone outsmarted by a Rubik's Cube. He opened the door and ran across the street, jumping over the puddles in which the lights from the shop fronts were reflected. She hadn't asked what he was up to, and he hadn't said. A cheeseburger was more interesting to her than him.

In truth, Sarge hardly knew himself what he was going to do. When he'd been searching for his cuff keys in that almighty screw up of a day, he'd come across another set of keys and almost without thinking had slipped them into his pocket. No one had noticed. That was before the news had got round and laughter had started up like frogs at dusk. Even the forensic people who never laughed at anything, had spluttered into their face masks as they passed by. It was much later that the idea came to him.

The first key worked, and he took this as a good sign. Wood splinters still lay on the floor, it didn't look as if anyone had bothered to tidy up since the raid. Unwashed plates had forks stuck to them like broken clock faces and a pale grey-brown liquid lurked in the bottom of the mugs that covered every surface. He half-expected an eye to suddenly open in the middle of the drying liquid. Socks were discarded on the floor like silhouette feet at nursery school showing the route.

The unfairness of life was brought home to him even more starkly. Why was his luck so shite when others who worked at nothing, sailed on without a care? And what was he even doing there, putting what was left of his career at risk? Sarge slumped to the floor with his head in his hands.

Recently there had been blood in his piss, and he knew this was a sign his disease was progressing. He referred to it as *his* rather than *the* disease because it was the only thing he really owned. It was like a coldblooded pet, something that returned no affection, yet he carried on talking to it and feeding it. There was medication he should be taking now but wasn't. It would be an admission that the long slow decline was gathering pace.

Sarge rubbed his eyes; he didn't want Rebecca to see him like this. She would move in for the kill, it was what she was waiting for. Sarge took a few deep breaths and pulled himself together.

It was as he was trying to work out how to get up, that he noticed the letter, which he had likely knocked to the floor. It made a little scout tent on the black and white lino. As he read it, he could hardly believe his luck and had to go over it several times to be sure. A broad smile slowly spread across his face. He would go to Mosque on Friday and give thanks.

This time getting up seemed to be easier than he reckoned. It didn't take long to spot the pen making a lone quill in the hedgehog pencil-holder.

With great care and trying to copy the existing handwriting as best he could, Sarge added another name to the list and placed the letter back where he guessed it should go.

***

When Jon returned with his sour cream Pringles and White Lightening, he knew immediately something was different. This was the second time. A disturbance in the micro-climate of dust hung in the air. After all, it was mostly his DNA, and the living space was in fact a living thing. The sofa was practically one of his organs. Absently, he toyed with the letter, re-reading the words written there.

If you're reading this, the bitch has killed me. Even if it looks like an accident, she murdered me. Avenge me!

And underneath was a list of names. He put the letter back and inch by inch searched the flat with his forehead torch.

Chapter 19

Empty sardine tins lay scattered around with their tops curled open and a

dull documentary about a stately home was playing in the background. An elderly woman who was dressed as if about to embark on a round of golf between the wars was pointing out a painting of a plump horse and red-faced rider. But it was the midget-sized armour with disproportionately big feet that had caught Jon's attention.

"They probably needed them for balance," Jon said.

"Like toys with weighted bottoms you can't knock over. Just think 1066, Agincourt, Bosworth – all the hacked off limbs twitching like fish in the mud and the bucking horses with cue ball eyes made by dwarfs running at each other with clown feet."

Jon turned to Ally, but Ally wasn't there. He would never be there again nor would anyone else.

"A gloss can be put on any amount of butchery given enough time."

Jon's voice trailed off to a whisper. It was the last programme he watched before putting his foot through the screen which popped.

***

Chicken fat hung in the air and a gang of youths blocked the pavement with their bikes as inseparable as a metal puzzle. A sapling had been snapped in half, but its leaves still retained their colour as it struggled on.

"I take Mum to see my dead brother," Sarge said. "She pats the ground and talks to him. She says, 'Sarge's here, come to see you.'"

"What do you say?"

"Nothing, he's dead," Sarge said. "She's used to not getting much back anyway."

The one time he'd gone to Islamabad, he'd felt out of place and was terrified of being kidnapped. There was loneliness and danger in such places, and also an impish glee in evil deeds. It was inescapable. He felt now his life was even more significant than back then and would be over soon.

"She gets flowers from the petrol station. The last time we went, it rained. The cemetery supplies golfing umbrellas in a bin. You just take one. She prayed and the rain hit the umbrella like impatient fingers tapping. I held it for both of us."

"And?"

"And nothing, that's just the way it was."

The bone-marrow light from the flat was even duller than usual, a bulb had most likely blown. It was frustrating nothing had happened since his break in, probably nothing ever would. What could you expect from someone who couldn't even change a lightbulb?

"A couple of workmen were on their phones, and one laughed a lot as if he was making a date."

Sarge leaned forward and started the Focus.

"The clay stuck to our shoes. It's hard to walk with clay on your feet."

***

When Jon tried the rifle, it sat snug in his shoulder. With his withered arm fully extended, his longest turkey finger could just reach the trigger. He'd inherited the .22 rifle from his father and it had a homemade magnetic eye patch on the side. Jon had moved to phase two, relocating to the lockup, smashing his mobile and wiping the laptop. He sat under camouflage netting in a fishing chair. It was lone wolf, comms-down mode. Next to his rucksack, he'd laid out army ration packs, water purifying tablets, a torch, hunting knife, sleeping bag, batteries, a Mars bar and candle stubs. This was it, zombie killing time. Then he decided it was OK to eat the Mars.

***

Ally woke drenched in sweat. Recently the dream was always the same: a statue as tall as the church it was on top of had the face of a badly painted gnome. It stiffly scanned the burnt-out buildings and ruins of some worn-torn state as citizens hurried through the chapel door. From the statue's head, a stubby tree grew like coral. As darkness fell, the tree became a lantern held aloft and the statue of St Francis peering into the gloom. From the church roof, he would bend forward to check one last time the dark streets for lost souls. Ally was huddled in a corner and wanted to cry out, but the arc of light always fell just short of him as it swept by.

Ally would've told Jon about his dream, but his previous life seemed far away now, and at last, he had something to look forward to. Maggie had brought back a scan that looked like a smoke-damaged lithograph and although it was difficult to make out anything much, Ally had an unfamiliar warm feeling.

***

Jon rechecked his equipment and there were two items of sentiment. His book of poems and an ESB stick with a single email from his father. It had been a warning not to forward on unsolicited emails but had requested the recipient send this to 10 friends. He had been one of his dad's friends, but Jon had never had anyone to pass it on to. The line stopped with him. Flicking through the book he chose a page at random:

> *The drink is drunk*
> *And the candle burned*
> *I won*

But there was nothing left
Everyone had gone.

Chapter 20

The boat rocked and smoke rose to lacquer another coat on the already deeply tanned ceiling. The light from the lamp seemed to stick to things like chewing gum. Rikki had just left. She was tall and strong and had manoeuvred him as if hefting an axe. She'd ridden off down Hoogte Kadijk, the sun filtering through her dress and showing off her fatless physique. After the last police visit, he'd run.

There was no guilt, well no one had died. Apart from Fran, of course, but what did that matter? She'd been dead for years and what he did was just to move her underground. After all, she'd been trying to do it herself for years and failing, he'd just helped her succeed for once in her miserable life. It'd been no more than exorcising a particularly persistent poltergeist. And Maggie was lost. Having gone native, she was playing house with Brain Dead. No, his plans couldn't have been much more of a disaster if he'd sabotaged them himself.

Then when things were at their darkest, a miracle had come along. A forgotten aunt who'd been festering away in Eastbourne had died and left him the small inheritance with which he bought the barge. It looked like a crusted sea chest broken open on the bank except all that spilled out was a rust and dirty laundry. Yet he liked the listing wreck and he really liked Amsterdam. For the most part. The only thing that really bothered him was that the Dutch were far too content. They'd never had to fight for anything, not tooth and nail like he had, and it made the children of the enchanted garden too damn smug for his liking.

He hadn't painted in months now and in truth, it had probably been years since he'd applied himself seriously. There was the realisation that he had no real vision. Greg just hadn't put the time in to develop a philosophy, he'd just reacted to his surroundings and when there was nothing to react to, he was lost. He'd stand for hours, his paints and canvassing waiting for him to start. They even seemed to sigh as if bored. But his mind would be empty, and his hand would jerk back at the last second with not a mark made on white space. Then he'd topple over the easel and scatter the paints and brushes aside. What surprised him most after he'd calmed down was how little he really missed painting and how lightly he carried the disappointment.

The boat rocked again like someone stepping on or off the deck. Perhaps Rikki had forgotten something, but the only things she ever seemed to carry with her were silence and the see-through dress that a single tug of the bow sent drifting to the floor. She never had or seemed to need money and Greg had the feeling he wasn't the only man she would visit in a day. His glass was empty, and a bottle rolled past. Lazily he stroked his chest where the hair was as coarse and dark as surgical stitches. He watched without alarm an ocular reflection transverse across the wall and then the table to finally come rest on the back of his hand. The last thing he heard was the snap of the porthole glass as if by a sudden frost, and the last thing he saw was the eruption of a bright red geyser from his chest.

***

Sarge stood shivering with his hands covering his genitals. The speedos he hadn't worn since he was 14 rode up his crack, and even back then, they were tight. Even the smallest sounds echoed loudly in a swimming pool and the chlorine reminded him of the mortuary he had to sometimes visit to pick up evidence. If anyone ever thought swimming was fun, they must be deluded, he thought. There was considerable splash and effort and the screams sounded like a waterboarding session. Rebecca was ploughing up and down in a diarrhoea-coloured costume, while fat men hung around in towelling-robes like swingers. White people seemed to have no shame about their bodies that they were like an expensive cheese that smelt bad, and no one really liked.

More to hide himself than an eagerness to get in, Sarge tiptoed over to the edge of the pool. It didn't look very inviting. He imagined the water washing around the backsides of all the people already in the pool. Telling himself he was to keep his face out of the water no matter what, Sarge gingerly lowered himself in. It came up to his chest before his feet touched the bottom. Bouncing on his toes, he made his way over to a corner. What was he meant to do next? Swimmers came up and tumble-turned in one inelegant movement. It had been more fun watching Bollywood films with his brother. He had been his happiest with his dying brother.

Another wave rolled by like a plump buttock.

Suddenly, Rebecca surged up next to him. Water slid smoothly off her cap and goggles giving the impression that she was melting. The poo costume was glossy like a fresh turd, and her breasts bobbed inches away from his face. She looked him up and down.

"I could've been an Olympic swimmer if I had put my mind to it," she said.

And I could've been George Clooney.

And then she was off again, legs thrashing, arms rotating and her chunky body barrelling from side to side as she breathed. It was nothing like the smooth rhythm the swimmers had on TV.

***

Jon was face-down in a crude nest of twigs and ivy which was wrapped around through the plant pot on his head. The empty pill box was made of brown plastic and had a white lid that clacked when turned. There was no knowing if the sleeping tablets would even still work. They'd been his mother's and must've been over twenty years old. It was the last of his meagre inheritance.

As Jon ran through the last few weeks, he couldn't believe everything had gone so smoothly. He'd discovered when he'd shot Maggie that a head didn't explode like a watermelon as in *The Day of the Jackal*, but the bullet was absorbed like sucking on a lozenge. It just sort of slurped out of sight. Afterwards, the blimp she'd been with had stood around unable to work out what was going on.

Done up in a Mack and trilby with a scarf over his face, he was like the *Invisible Man* or someone allergic to sunlight. Either would do. He had even looked up as if he'd been shat on by a seagull. What a sap. Even tracking down Greg had been easy, 50 pence and 30 mins at the internet café had found his Facebook page. The boat name was clearly visible as he'd held a bottle of beer up to the camera. The gun he'd packed with fishing rods in a rucksack and taken the ferry, which didn't seem to have any security. No one stopped or bothered to search him.

Jon rubbed his eye. Dogshit in a bag hung from a branch above him. It looked soft to the touch and made him think of Ally's story about the amputee and his drainage pouch. He blinked and squinted through the sights again. Figures sat in the sun. They were red in the face and he could hear bursts of coarse laughter. They lay next to him and he flicked through it. One page had a corner a turned over which he couldn't remember doing. It opened at a poem called *You were Happy that Day*.

> *You were happy that day*
> *Slipping past me to lead the way*
> *Your feet sunk into the dunes*
> *And we had coffee at the Skyliner café.*
> *The generator hummed*
> *And fried onions hung in the air.*
> *You said it reminded you of the fair coming*
to town

Dangerous men and the reek of unleavened
sex.

    On the beach we saw two seals
    With Smurf-shaped heads and bright eyes
    They watched us and you took my hand.
    In the dunes I gave you the photo of my
mum.

    Her hat was pulled down
    And she held her handbag in front of her.
    You said she looked like a squaw woman
    Recently but not securely converted to
Christianity.

    You could put things like that.
    Afterwards I could see her breaking free one
full moon
    And going crazy with a kitchen knife.

Jon closed the book. It had been a day trip to Great Yarmouth before the Greek waiter. The sea had been dark like iron filings and the crew of a skiff were straining with every pull on the oars but still they were pushed back. Yet it been the best day of his life, one when he'd felt the same as everyone else.

***

Forty minutes later and Sarge was sipping his first ever G & T. Most of his cousins drank secretly in their parents' car, eating chicken in a box and sharing a spliff. It's where they hid from the wives they took for granted. Watching the tennis reminded him of Miss Joan Hunter Dunn from Mr Wright's English class. He absently flicked at flies and the alcohol blazed inside him. After the game, sweating members of the police social club slapped each other on the back and adopted poses from Grand Theft Auto, their rackets makeshift Uzis. Sarge reckoned it was the sort of place where the East End working class and minor aristocracy could rub shoulders to indulge in a shared weakness for fascism and rent boys. A bluebottle settled on the rim of his glass and rubbed its hands in glee.

Who the hell had invited him anyway, Rebecca thought, sitting there in his white shorts but hadn't played a single game? It was impossible to know what he was thinking as he hadn't said a damn word. In the pool, he'd been like a splashed nancy. Yet he'd still managed to stare at her nipples sticking through her costume. She slowly sipped a Pimm's and wiped her face with the towel round her neck. Let him stare. She had to admit he looked good with his brown hairy legs, like Vijay Amritraj in that James Bond film she could never remember the title of. He gave the club a colonial air.

Rebecca took out a cigarette without taking her eyes off him. She knew it would annoy him. Waving his hand in front of his face like an old spinster flapping an antimacassar to get rid of dust. He would learn the laws of the land didn't apply here. Nothing could touch them here. She clicked away at a lighter with her thumb methodically like a band leader counting in the next number, but it stubbornly refused to work. After many attempts it caught, and she tilted her head back to let a mushroom cloud of smoke roll heavenwards.

Sweat trickled down her thighs and she felt as if insects were crawling around her gusset. The heat was becoming unbearable. On top of everything, a red spot had started to dart over the table and her dress. It was probably some fat prick, CID tosser, pissing around with a laser pen.

Her brief acceptance of Sarge's presence passed as quickly as it had come – just what was he looking so fucking happy about? What the hell was he even doing there? It was an unspoken rule that the club was the last outpost of apartheid. She closed her legs and buried her face in the towel. There was brief respite in its cool dampness, and she took the moment to breathe the air deeply into her lungs. As she let the towel drop, she saw Sarge's eyes eager as a hunting dog's and his tongue moistening his lips. Then a brilliant new galaxy exploded in her head and in that self-same instant shrunk back to leave a dark and impenetrable nothingness.

***

The irregular coin-sized circle that suddenly appeared on Rebecca's forehead was like a wax seal. Pandemonium erupted around Sarge, men squatted in loose shorts and on some, their gonads hung out like poisonous fruit. They pointed to the rolling hills up to the left and phones were snapped open. No one noticed Sarge quietly slip away.

Dusk was gathering and the turbines on the Ferryboatman Industrial Estate lethargically churned the evening air. Death came as assuredly to the healthy as it did to the sick, sooner or later it came. Arshad had lived with his sickness for a long time, and in the end had got used to it like a badly fitting shoe. Sarge reached country lanes and trees either side of the road arched over him. He neither knew nor cared where he was headed. Just above his head bats wriggled energetically through the gathering gloom.

The steady pulse of life that flowed through the beech trees filled Sarge with a strength he hadn't felt in years. There was a recycling process, and eventually his atoms would become part of the quiet and unassuming things. But not today, for his would be a slow fall. Today he was alive, the scent of flowers filled his lungs, and Sarge's step was more joyful than any of those whose seemingly endless lives stretched out before them.

Printed in Great Britain
by Amazon